Ticity

By: Jennie Stiglic

Editor: Cathy Zitnik

DEDICATION

To my family and friends:
Thank you for not laughing when I said I was going to write a novel!

To my students – past, present and future:
This story is for you. I see your superpower.

The Strengths:
Ticity

CHAPTER 1

Jalyn

Jalyn was lying in her bed looking around her bedroom desperately trying to fall asleep. This had become a nightly struggle for the Westwood High junior. As an honor student and class officer, life was very big for her right now. Combined with upcoming college testing, volleyball season, and prom planning, her mind was racing 100 miles an hour.

Jalyn knew what her future would look like, and everything she did now was critical to making her goals a reality. She, and her parents, had spent her high school years meticulously planning her every move, and so far everything was on track, at least that is what her parents told her. Of course, in order to keep this pace it took everything she had...actually, truth be told...it took more than what she had. And she knew in her heart there was no room for mistakes. In the end, though, she knew it would all be worth it - all the sacrifices, all the hours studying, all the sleepless nights, and all the times she chose to focus on school instead of hanging out with friends - it would be all worth it when she became a successful pediatrician after attending one of the most prestigious universities.

Jalyn sat desperately trying to get some rest, but her mind felt like it was being bombarded by a cosmic explosion of ideas, and she could not calm her thoughts. "Ugh, maybe if I looked through my to-do list one more time, then I will be able to sleep," Jalyn convinced herself.

She pulled open her phone and scrolled through the list:

Tomorrow:

1. Class officer meeting before school
   - Set-up date for food tasting for prom
   - Decide on a theme
   - Pick out decorations within two weeks so they arrive in time
2. Tutor Maddie during first-period study hall

3. Sell flowers for homecoming week for the honor society

4. 7th period: viola sectionals

5. After school: volleyball game, orchestra concert, Fresco's, study for...everything!

Suddenly, Jalyn's heart stopped. "Crap, I forgot to text Ethan back with help on the history homework. Shoot! Shoot! Shoot! He's going to be so pissed! Stupid me!"

She jumped up to grab her history homework out of her backpack and frantically typed a response to Ethan with a picture of the answers he needed. Just as she hit send, a message popped up, and she could see that the class officers had been going back and forth earlier this evening about prom theme ideas.

She sat back and scrolled through their messages. "Let me think...Joey wants a medieval/knight theme, Missy wants a fairytale theme, and Kiesha wants a garden theme. Hmmm...I'm sure there is something I can come up with that will make everyone happy. Let's see...let's see." Jalyn spent the next 30 minutes searching the Internet for ideas. Finally, she was certain she found the perfect idea. She went on the group chat and started typing, "Hey, why don't we do a cinema-themed prom? Something like a movie night in the park. We can decorate using movie themes, so we can have different areas decorated as medieval, fairytale, and garden themes but we would just tie the overall theme to various movie genres. What do you think?"

Without waiting for a response, Jalyn turned off her phone pretty confident she had just nailed the perfect theme idea that would make everyone happy. By now her stomach was growling and tightening from hunger. She knew she had to fall asleep before it got too bad. Hesitantly, she reached into her bag, took a deep breath, and popped one of her mom's pills. She relaxed knowing sleep was on the way to find her.

Ethan

"What a jerk! I hate this! I hate him! Why do I even bother with this??!!" Ethan thought to himself as he sat alone in the corner booth of China Star waiting for the person he calls "Dad" to meet him for dinner. Ethan had about a 30/70 chance that his dad would even show up. He ran his hands through his hair and brought his elbows down to the table with a thump. He had already been waiting for over an hour, and he could feel the blood rushing to his face and his fists getting sweaty and ready to punch something. The waiter came to his table for the third time to refill his water glass. "Would you like to order, sir?" the waiter asked, a little more direct this time.

"Do you think I want to order now? I told you already that I am waiting for someone? This place is half empty anyway. Seriously! What the hell?" Ethan could feel his heart pounding as the anger built up inside. The waiter walked away stunned. Ethan sat red-faced and ready to punch a hole in the wall. He got up to leave just as the door to the restaurant opened, and his dad walked in.

"Ethan, my son, give your dad a hug. It's great to see you!" his dad said as he hobbled over to the table where Ethan was waiting. Before his dad could actually hug him, he leaned over and grabbed his phone. He put his finger up indicating to Ethan that he had to take what looked like an important call.

"Ethan, just one second. I need to take this," his dad said as he leaned slightly away from him in an air of arrogance. "No, put it all on the Reds to win. Yes, I'm sure - all of it. I know, I know they're not favored to win. Just means a bigger payout in the end," he let out a quick laugh as he hung up the phone. Ethan knew this routine all too well. His dad was always gambling or betting on horse races, sporting games, anything that could be a quick payout for him. "OK, where were we?" his dad asked, oblivious to Ethan's mood.

"Well, I was sitting here for an hour already waiting for you…" His dad interrupted Ethan without hesitation, barely noticing Ethan's frustration. "Oh, before I forget to tell you, I have a new place I am staying in."

Ethan willed his anger to lessen a bit. He would never admit it to himself, but deep down, while he hated how his dad treated him with every ounce of his soul, he always felt a twinge of relief those times when his dad would actually show up.

"The place I am staying in is a huge house with an in-ground pool, tennis courts, and awesome hot tub. I am actually staying in the guest house, but still, it's amazing." His dad grabbed a roll and continued to eat and talk, barely looking up at Ethan. "Not too bad for your old man. Maybe you can come some time and visit?" His dad switched topics once again without even taking a breath. "Let's order. I'm starving," he said.

Ethan knew the drill. Every visit from his dad was pretty much the same. He was the most self-absorbed person Ethan had ever known. Every visit left Ethan with so much hate in his heart. If it weren't for the occasional gifts and stuff his dad gave him, he wouldn't even bother with the old guy...at least that is what he told himself.

As Ethan opened his menu, he glanced at the brace on his dad's leg, almost too afraid to ask. "So what happened to your leg?"

"Well, you see, the guy that owns the guest house I am staying at backed into me with his car last week in a parking lot. It was terrible, and I still don't know how he didn't see me behind him." Ethan got a pit in his stomach hearing what he knew was a lie. "After insisting on calling the cops, I told him about my struggle to find a place to live, how I have been on disability, and how I have to support you..." Ethan almost threw up in his mouth. His dad hadn't given his mom a dime in years. He is about as deadbeat as a dad could get, but he could pull a scam better than anyone. His dad continued, "When I was done talking, the guy basically begged me to stay in his guest house until I got back on my feet." He winked at Ethan with a knowing look, and Ethan knew all too well what that look meant. He felt a knot of hate, anger, and sadness in his stomach as he looked at his dad. This was the same feeling that would creep up in Ethan's stomach when he would look at his own image in a mirror.

Maddie

"Holy headache! Wow!" Maddie rolled over to see her friends sleeping in various places and positions around the living room floor. "Man, last night was epic!" she thought to herself. Thank goodness for Rob's parents' last-minute trip to New York. No parents meant fun times with her friends. Maddie loved these times more than anything, and alcohol definitely helped get the party started.

She closed her eyes and slowly the events of last night came back to her memory. They had started the evening off the way they always did by shot-gunning a beer. Once the festivities started, she spent most of her time with her best friends dancing, laughing, and mingling with the crowd. This was the best part of her week. She felt so free, so calm, talking and socializing with her friends and classmates. If only she could freeze time and keep life this way.

Even though her head was pounding, her heart was happy. She loved the times she could shake off the stress of her world, and just be herself. She was a natural with others and could seamlessly navigate social situations, actually, most situations. She remembered her conversation with Ethan last night. "Ethan is such an ass," she flinched as if she was back in the moment with him, "and for no reason. It is almost like his goal is to make people hate him." Her mind sank as she remembered their conversation.

He had come up to her at the party oozing charm and was bragging about how he had gotten a keg of beer off his dad for the party. He wouldn't shut up about it. Like his dad was some hero or something. As he leaned in closer to Maddie, she could smell the stench of alcohol and cigarettes on his breath as he said, "You can pay me back with a kiss. You know you want to..." He then reached his hand behind her back. Maddie couldn't help it, she busted out laughing, accidentally spitting some beer in Ethan's face. She didn't mean to, but his face was so, so, so smug and omg - it was hilarious. Of course, the humor of the situation could have been the hit she took off of Tommy, but still, was he serious?! Ethan did not think it was funny. He grabbed her beer away from her, and stared right into her eyes, "Your loss, bitch." Maddie had no idea what he was going to do. "I am taking your beer. Besides, we all know you are too stupid to know what is good for you anyway." He emphasized the word 'stupid.' This hard slap of reality hurt and knocked Maddie right off her high. She almost wished he had actually hit her. Nothing hurt more than that awful, horrible, terrible word!

Maddie pushed back the tears and closed her eyes one more time hoping to erase the memory of Ethan and remember more of the good parts of last night, and maybe, magically make time stand still. She looked around the room and a warm feeling filled her heart as she looked at all her friends. She loved Friday and Saturday nights with her friends, but today was now Sunday...and she hated Sundays. She knew at some point she would have to go home.

In an attempt to make the morning last, Maddie got up, freshened up in the bathroom, and made breakfast. She paused to look at herself in the mirror. Maddie had always been confident with her looks, and she knew that while she was not some amazing beauty, she had always loved her effortless wavy brown hair and clear, olive complexion. Her appearance, like her friendships, seemed to come naturally to her. She smiled and bounced happily into the kitchen.

Maddie enjoyed cooking and trying out new recipes. But today, she knew everyone would love a nice, greasy breakfast. In fact, she was fairly famous amongst Westwood High party-goers for her signature breakfast that people affectionately called Maddiecakes. It was her own blend of pancake batter with cinnamon and avocado to help with the hangovers. Surprisingly baked in the center was perfectly cooked eggs, bacon and whatever vegetables she could find. She also had her own special sauce to put on top, a recipe she never shared with anyone. The smell of her Maddiecakes slowly woke her friends from their groggy sleep. She dished out the pancakes onto plates and handed them to thankful party-goers.

After everyone was stuffed and the house was put back in order, there was no place to go but home. Maddie searched for any reason not to have to get in her car and head back, but there was none.

She knew her parents meant well and were always there cheering her on. They were beyond committed to her success and put everything they had behind her - literally everything. But that was the problem and the cause of her perpetual weekday chest pain.

As she pulled the car into the driveway, Maddie already knew what she would find once she walked through that door. Her parents would be there at the kitchen table ready to make sure she was doing her homework, reminding her to practice her pitching, asking her what tests she had coming up that week. Blah...blah...blah. "We let you be with friends on the weekend," they would remind her, "and you work hard on school and softball the rest of the time. We have a deal, right?" That's what they always said. The warmth in Maddie's heart was being replaced with the all-too-familiar weight that usually sat right on her chest pressing the air out of her lungs and happiness out of her heart. She had promised her parents that she would work hard with her tutors to keep her grades up so colleges would look at her for a softball scholarship. It was her junior year, and apparently, this was an important time for her to focus and work hard. Her parents were always telling her how expensive college was, and she knew that her parents were not exactly rolling in the dough. So, it was her job to get a scholarship in order to pay for school. She knew this all too well. It's all she knew. It was all she heard. She might as well have a tutor strapped to her side. It was the only thing keeping her afloat in school.

School would be absolutely unbearable if it weren't for sports. Maddie loved softball. Like head-over-heels loved it. She had been playing since she was three years old, and nothing was better than having that cap on her head, some dirt on her hand, staring down the batter waiting to throw the perfect pitch to send them back to the dugout. She felt alive on the softball field with a little sun on her arms and crowds cheering from the grass...at least she *used* to feel this way. Now it was this big, gigantic thing in her life. As soon as she had some success in softball, the bar got raised. No matter what...her performance, her pitches, her hitting...it could always get better. At first, Maddie loved the challenge. She loved seeing if she could throw farther or hit harder. But then softball took on a life of its own. Her parents and coaches and teammates and private coaches were expecting her to be perfect, college perfect. Everyone was putting all their energy and effort into her, and while she appreciated it, it was a lot of weight to carry. Her coaches saw a chance to "coach" a player into the big league. Maddie's parents could finally see hope that their little girl could be college-bound because, let's face it, Maddie had earned a reputation for being less than spectacular in school.

They all cared about her so much and she did not want to let them down. They were all working so hard for her. But, man, if only she could just get this massive pressure off her chest. Her mind snapped back into the moment, and she could barely breathe. The stress was back full force.

CHAPTER 2

Jalyn

"Hey, babe, thanks for the history homework," Ethan winked at Jalyn in the hallway.

In her head, Jalyn knew he was a total player, albeit a hot player, but the fact that he was happy because of something she had done...well, that added a little bounce to her step and enhanced her already good mood.

Her morning was off to a fantastic start. The class officer meeting went really well. Everyone loved her theme idea for senior prom. Of course, she now had 8 more things to do since they decided on a prom theme, but she figured she would just add them to her bottomless to-do list. Tutoring with Maddie was good. Maddie always had a smile on her face, and even though she has no idea what she is doing in geometry (or any of her other subjects), she's always thankful for her help. No wonder she is one of the most popular girls in school. Not only is she beyond beautiful, but you can't help but be drawn to her contagious smile and positive attitude. She just seems to have such a happiness about her, and she always seems so ready to focus on other people. Most students at Westwood High are more focused on themselves and trying to figure out the crazy world of high school. As Jalyn zoned out into a world where she was as beautiful and content as Maddie, the bell rang for history class to start.

Mr. Rotiger was lecturing on World War I and asking who could summarize the three main points from last night's reading. Right on cue, the rest of the class started desperately studying their books or looking off in any direction but at the teacher. As if the answers would just magically pop out of the pages like one of those 3D greeting cards. Jalyn looked around, knowing she would be the only one fully prepared for today's (and every day's) class. She rolled her eyes and raised her hand, Mr. Rotiger smiled and pointed to her. "Ah, Miss Chibuzo, I always know I can count on you." Jalyn spent the next three minutes eloquently detailing the key points from last night's chapters. When she finished, Mr. Rotiger clapped with praise for her answer. Jalyn blushed in her seat thrilled for this well-deserved approval. That extra hour of studying was really paying off now!

Just then she noticed Ethan catch her eye with a combined look of awe and annoyance. Jalyn's confidence vanished into worry. She hated this part. If you tried too hard in school then the teachers were happy, and the students were annoyed. Jalyn was always searching for the perfect combination of effort and avoiding being annoying. Making other people happy seemed so impossible sometimes! How was she supposed to know what everyone else wanted? That question was always on Jalyn's mind, along with the perpetual pang in her stomach. They were always there flicking away at her self-esteem. Flick. Flick. Flick. How was she supposed to make all these fickle people around her happy?! Just as she started to obsess about this, the pencil sharpener jolted her back into the class, and she buried the nervous feeling next to the pit in her stomach. Jalyn shook herself back into her normal, outwardly-confident self.

The rest of the school day went great. She felt like she was on fire. During the volleyball game after school, Jalyn served for 5 points helping her team beat the Patriots in two games. Then she nailed her solo at orchestra rehearsal. She was on cloud 9 when she headed to dinner with her family. They had their weekly dinner at Fresco's, their favorite Italian restaurant in town. Her whole family was there: her dad, the orthodontist, her mom, who manages a medical practice in town, her brother, and grandparents. Her mom had always been the business-minded one of the family. Their big joke was Mom could manage a checkbook better than Dad, but Dad knew how to make people smile. Dorky, right?! Her brother, Leno, happened to be home from college this week. He was away at school studying to be an orthopedic surgeon. They were a family of medical and business gurus. Yep, all of them. Even her grandparents fit into this category. They had started their own small grocery business shortly after coming to this country, and now it was one of the largest stores in the region; there had even been talks of launching new stores nationwide.

Her mom spent the first 10 minutes of dinner bragging about Jalyn's straight A average, her success in volleyball, and even told them that she planned on running for class president next year. Jalyn smiled just like she was supposed to do, but all she could think was that the entire family was well aware of all of these points, but bragging about her kids was just what Jalyn's mom always did. Her mom continued,

"This of course means that Jalyn will be delivering the coveted speech at graduation! I am just so excited for her!" Her mom beamed with pride as she looked at her perfect daughter. Jalyn knew the speech was so important to her mom because that is what she did at her high school graduation. "Who knows, Jalyn could be the most successful one out of all of us. With her grades and SAT scores...the sky's the limit for you, Jalyn." Jalyn gave her perfected good-girl smile and nodded.

But just then, her grandfather jumped in, "Jalyn, what do you want to study in college? What is your passion?" Jalyn knew the correct answer to this question and responded just like her parents had ingrained into her brain, "I want to become a pediatrician. I can't wait to work in the medical field." A roar came from the depths of Jalyn's stomach as it growled in hunger. It growled as if to yell at her, knowing more than she did about her reality. She wasn't sure if it was hunger for food or a hunger for something else. She had to cough to cover up the sound. She knew she was starving, but she had trained her mind to ignore this hunger inside of her. Almost in response to the growl, dinner was delivered to the table, and Jalyn started eating her spaghetti, loving every single bite of dripping noodles, tasty sauce, and warm meat that she put into her mouth. She closed her eyes to savor the taste as the food filled her stomach and drowned the uneasy feelings, stopping them from surfacing again until later.

What an amazing feeling! She couldn't help but share her happiness. "This spaghetti is amazingly delicious. Oh my gosh!"

"Relax, you get it every week," her brother teased. Jalyn stuck her tongue out at him, and they just laughed.

These were the moments she savored because she knew this full stomach and calm family time was just temporary. The warm food in her stomach was like a soft blanket on a cold winter's night, but it did not matter. Her weight was exactly the size her mom told her was perfect for her height, and she had the tools to keep it that way. There was that word again, perfect. It followed Jalyn wherever she went, constantly sitting on her shoulder just waiting for the moment she faltered. She wanted to savor this moment of contentment, but ultimately control was more important. Jalyn needed to be in control. She craved this control: control over her appearance, control over her actions, control over anything she could.

Once dinner was done, she excused herself to go to the bathroom. It was time to make things right. After checking all the stalls to make sure they were empty, Jalyn purged...everything. The comfort of food in her belly was replaced with the feeling of success as she regained control of the food she had eaten. She did not even need to put her finger in her throat, she could make herself throw up by just squeezing her stomach muscles. It was a powerful feeling. "Others may say this was a bad habit," she thought, "or eating disorder?" It wasn't a disorder if she had it under control, right? One time at school, a girl caught her throwing up in the bathroom during lunch and reported her to the counselor. After having to listen to the lecture, Jalyn convinced the counselor that she had just not felt well and most definitely did not have an eating disorder. "Eating disorder?" she laughed to herself. It's not a disorder at all. In fact, it was an amazing tool for success. She could eat the foods she wanted but still maintain her perfect body.

When she was done, Jalyn wiped off her mouth, and reached into her purse for mouthwash and eye drops. She rinsed with some mouthwash, put some drops in her eyes, and patted down her shirt near her stomach. She looked in the mirror and smiled. She knew she was winning!

Ethan

"Hunny, hunny, it's time to wake up. Ethan…"

"Leave me alone! Go away! Stay away!" Ethan screamed at his mom as she flinched and moved backwards into the hallway.

"Ethan, it's time to get up for school. I made you your favorite chocolate chip pancakes for breakfast," his mom continued.

"Whatever," he muttered and threw on the closest shirt and shorts he could find. Ethan stumbled into the bathroom to brush his teeth, looked in the mirror, and frowned. "Screw you," was all he could say to the reflection looking back at him. Ethan's self-loathing was all he knew. He had so much anger inside of him with no idea how to get rid of it. By now he knew there was no reason to waste time thinking about it. Ethan shook off the uneasy feeling, went downstairs to eat the pancakes his mom made, and left without saying a word to her. "She just sits at her desk with her computer drinking her coffee anyway," he said to himself. Ethan dismissed the guilt that threatened to enter his mind and drove off in his beat-up old Mustang just like he always did.

His dad sucks, but at least he got him this Mustang in some sleaze ball poker game, or at least that is what Dad had told Ethan happened. It could be stolen for all Ethan knew.

As Ethan parked in an illegal spot by the auto class at Westwood High, he looked in the mirror, slicked back his hair, and knew it was time. "Let's do this!" Ethan gave a sideways smile to a girl who walked past him as he shut the door and headed into school.

The best part about high school classes for Ethan was there was always a goody-goody, or try-hard, in all of his classes. All he had to do was smile and charm them a little bit, and BAM, they were like putty in his hands. It was almost too easy.

In his first period class, there was Hannah. She did almost all of Ethan's math homework, and all he had to do was to pretend to be soooo confused, compliment her hair, and just like that...answers to his math questions. Second period history class was even easier. There was this girl named Jalyn who basically got off on just showing the world how smart she was. She was the biggest pushover of them all.

Everything was smooth sailing that day until homeroom with Maddie. Ethan had been avoiding Maddie after the horrible situation at the party this weekend. She had blown Ethan off and then spit beer in his face. All he had done was try to kiss her. A very normal, high school activity. "All I wanted to tell her was that she was drinking beer thanks to me. She could have kissed me. After all, I was the one who worked my magic and guilted my dead-beat dad into buying me a keg. She should have been thankful and impressed, but instead, she laughed in my face. I didn't deserve that kind of treatment," he thought to himself. Ethan's plan was to just blow her off and make her come crawling back to apologize to him. Ethan thought this plan was working like a charm because as soon as he walked into homeroom, she came straight over to him. But then she looked right at him and walked right past him.

"Whatever, bitch," Ethan muttered under his breath. Just then he noticed Maddie talking to some other classmates laughing. "Was she laughing at me?" Ethan thought to himself, squeezing his hands into fists.

Everything about this situation made Ethan feel incredibly uncomfortable, and he hated uncomfortable. Why was she not falling for his charm? That was his only go-to move. She probably saw the same thing he saw in himself - nothing. He knew he was a big joke; that's why they were laughing. All of this angered Ethan. His self-doubt started to rise to the surface and his face grew bright red. He hated himself. No! He hated all of his classmates. It was their fault. It was all their fault. He needed to escape. Escape his mind. Escape this room.

"Well, the joke would be on her," he recovered, "No one would make him look stupid. He was better than them anyway." He convincingly lied to himself.

"Hey, Teach, I am going to the bathroom," Ethan blurted out.

"Mr. Waltz, that is no way to speak to a teacher. Do you care to rephrase that?" Ethan could feel his emotions boiling over. He took a loud breath and walked closer to the teacher using every ounce of calm he had left and whispered, "May I please use the bathroom?"

When the teacher said yes, he ran out of the class as quickly as possible with his fists balled up next to him, anger ready to explode at any moment. Ethan walked into the bathroom, splashed water on his face, and wanted nothing more than to punch the damn mirror into a million pieces.

Maddie

The best parts of school were passing periods, lunch, and gym with friends. People always say their favorite class is lunch, but for Maddie, everything else was freakin' theater time. She had to pretend to know what she was doing in classes, figure out what to say to make teachers think she was understanding their lessons, and continuously look for new creative ways to say, "Yes, I understand. Yes, I will work on that." It was all bullshit because Maddie had no idea when she would need or use the information she learned in class. Nothing came easy to her, and every class felt like a slow march through thick sand. She spent most of her days thanking everyone for helping get her through this masquerade of school. But her gratitude was real. She was very grateful for her tutors and teachers, but as soon as she felt like she mastered some class content, they moved on to a new topic. So Maddie smiled and pretended while everyone around her tried to "fix" her. Put that on repeat and you have Maddie's life. Maddie only felt like herself during those rare times when she could hang out with friends. She felt happy and alive when she could just be herself away from the struggles of school.

Fortunately, she started most days in study hall with Jalyn as her tutor. They were not friends exactly, but Maddie needed her help, and Jalyn was incredibly smart. Jalyn was the picture of perfect:

perfect grades, perfect person, perfect plan for her future...perfect, perfect, perfect. Half the time Maddie sat staring at Jalyn completely baffled how one person could understand all of this nonsense, and half the time she wanted to hug Jalyn for working so hard to help her. Jalyn had taken her on as her pet project. It seemed like Maddie's success was somehow connected to Jalyn's happiness.

Each day after school, Maddie went to private softball pitching lessons, which used to be a great part of her day. Now, even this had become work. There were so many expectations for her to become this college pitcher, and it used to be her dream too. She loved softball and loved every aspect of the game, but now it was this impossible task she needed to master along with every other part of her life. There was little room for error or fun for that matter. Maddie always had to give 110%. Her parents were paying a ton of money for this top-notch coach to analyze every aspect of her pitching. Every inch of her movement was videotaped, reviewed, and discussed. After faking her way through school all day, this was not how Maddie wanted to spend her afternoons. Rather than having someone micro-analyze her every move, she wished she could just play the game, win or lose, just play!

As soon pitching lessons were over, Maddie always ran as fast as she could from the door to her room trying to avoid the attack of questions from her parents. Today she was not so lucky.

"How was school? How did you do on your geometry test? Coach said you are doing really well on your changeup. Maddie, don't walk away? We want to talk to you."

Maddie dodged their questions like bullets and ran to her room, "Gotta go. Sorry, Mom. Gotta do homework. Lots of studying to do!" She slammed her door shut, put on her earphones, and blasted her music. The weight of the world was back on her chest and heavier than ever. All she wanted to do was to escape, to run away from the impossible expectations and from the constant pressure she felt. But there was no escape. She couldn't let down everyone around her. They were working so hard to help make her successful. They were working so hard to help her compensate for her weaknesses, but did it really have to feel like this.

"I am worthless," Maddie thought, "I am no good. All these people want college so bad for me, and I have no way of actually pulling this off. I will never be what everyone wants me to be. I wish I wasn't so stupid. Why am I so stupid? I hate all of this. Ugh - what's wrong with me that I don't want the same things they do!? What's the use?! I wish... I wish I could just die. Disappear into nothingness... Just float away." Maddie sat there still shocked that she had even thought this. She didn't want to die. Of course she didn't. But she wanted to escape all this. She turned her music turned off and just pictured herself floating away. Away from school, away from sports, away from expectations - just floating away on a calm sea of water. Just that thought alone made her feel the weight release from her chest. She could breathe.

CHAPTER 3

Jalyn

Waking up to blurred vision and a foggy mind, she looked at the clock and screamed. It was 5:30 a.m.! Not only would she have to skip her morning workout, but today would have to be a dry shampoo and ponytail day if she was going to make it to school in time for the zero-hour Principal's Advisors Cabinet Meeting. Today was yet another busy day with another long list of to-dos. The sleeping pill she had stolen from her mom helped her sleep, but waking up the next morning was awful. All she wanted to do was rest, but she knew this was an impossible dream. So she slapped her face a few times, got up, and looked at herself in the mirror. She let her eyes fall to the corner of her mirror. There, tucked into the corner, was one of her family's favorite quotes, "If you're not first, you're last." That quote always gave Jalyn the nudge she needed to keep going.

Jalyn got ready quickly and headed downstairs as fast as she could.

She walked into the kitchen just as her dad was pouring his morning coffee.

"Ready for the day, my dear?" my dad asked her with a hug.

"Of course," she said with a feigned smile and a facade of happiness. "Just grabbing a quick bite before heading in for the Principal's Advisors Cabinet Meeting."

Her dad put his hands on her shoulders and smiled. "We are so proud of you. You are such a good girl. How did we get so lucky to have you?" He kissed her forehead and headed to the car to drive to work.

Despite a rough start to the morning, her dad's words helped Jalyn feel back in control of the day. Her stomach growled from the emptiness of last night's dinner. This too gave her some confidence that she was fully in charge of her life - even with a late start this morning. She finally headed to school after allowing herself to have half of an apple for breakfast.

The morning seemed to be on the up and up with a successful advisors meeting and a great conversation with the principal after the meeting. But once Jalyn made it to tutoring, Maddie seemed off...like really off. Normally, Maddie was one of the happiest people she knew, but today she was quiet and distant. She normally wore her hair in a carefree ponytail, but today her hair was down and clearly not brushed and her sweatshirt had a stain on the arm, which did not seem to bother her at all. After multiple attempts to boost Maddie's mood and, heck, she had even just given Maddie some of the answers to the geometry homework, Maddie snapped at Jalyn for no reason at all.

"You are nothing but a try-hard. Do you know that you annoy people with all your perfectness? Like really annoy people. Doesn't that bother you?" Maddie put her head in her hands, started crying, and quickly changed moods. "Just give up on me, Jalyn. I am begging you. Stop trying to help me."

Jalyn was speechless. She had never seen this side of Maddie, and she certainly was not one to handle drama.

Maddie looked at Jalyn with a look of desperation in her eyes. "You have absolutely no idea how I feel. How could you? Everything about you is perfect. You could not possibly know anything about the struggles that the rest of us have."

Maddie stormed off crying as Jalyn tried to tell her, "You're doing great. This is hard. I am here to help you." Jalyn knew her words sounded empty as they chased Maddie out the door and down the hall.

It was no use. Maddie was gone, and Jalyn was left feeling like a failure. Oh, right, a failure who annoys people. She sat there running the situation over and over in her mind. "What did I do wrong? Why is trying to be perfect a bad thing? I work really hard to do things the right way, real hard! Clearly, I did not work hard enough with Maddie. What could I have done better? Why was Maddie so angry at me? All I did was try and help?!" The bell rang, and Jalyn was still thinking about the situation as she headed into the hallway. She hated it when people did not like her. Suddenly, Ethan started waving to her from across the hall. Jalyn barely noticed him until he was right in front of her.

He was whispering the words, "Can I borrow your science homework?"

Shocker! Ethan always "needed" Jalyn for her homework. She was not in the mood for this right now, but what other option did she have. In a daze, she handed over her notebook and attempted to make eye contact the best she could. She covered her feelings with the smile she could so easily paint on her lips. "I need that back by lunch, Ethan."

"You're the best. You know that, right, Jalyn?" Ethan gave her a little hug.

She could barely feel her arms. She felt like she was in slow motion. "No problem. Happy to help," Jalyn robotically replied to Ethan as he smiled and walked away.

Jalyn's mind was spinning out of control. Her classes were a blur, and lunch offered a slight distraction because she was selling homecoming flowers, but all she could see was Maddie sitting there at lunch with her friends barely talking at all. What was Maddie talking about this morning? Jalyn had struggles. She struggled to come up with good school spirit events, and she struggled to figure out the best sales ideas for homecoming? She struggled to decide if she would run for president of the honor society or class president. Being class president meant giving the prestigious speech at graduation. That would be her crowning jewel for senior year. "See, I have struggles!" Jalyn said aloud to no one in particular as her stomach let out a growl.

She was still struggling with her thoughts about Maddie when she headed to English class. She took a deep breath and forced herself to put Maddie out of her mind. Jalyn loved everything about this class...the writing, the stories, the creativity...and she would not let Maddie's drama about Jalyn being perfect ruin it. Of course, her family thought that, aside from the writing, the rest of the class was not really of value in the "real world." She heard this from her parents every time she went on and on about the heroic or tragic stories they were reading in class. Her parents felt that math and science classes were better suited for a successful medical career versus classes in the arts. The most important thing about English, to them, was that A+ printed on her report card.

As soon as she entered Mrs. Ozark's class, she knew immediately it was a conference day in class. Mrs. Ozark always conferenced with students after they wrote papers for her. It was her chance to give them feedback and guidance on their writing. Jalyn was one of the first students to get called to conference. She loved these days! Her English teachers always had great feedback for her and praised her strong writing skills. English was so different from her other classes. She loved every minute of the work she did for English versus the other classes where she had to spend hours and hours studying. English class had homework, but it felt more like an escape than work. This was exactly what she needed to change her day around.

The conference started off great. "Jalyn, I was very much looking forward to talking with you about the fictional story you wrote. Now here, let me take you through some of the suggestions I have to improve your story..." Mrs. Ozark continued, but all Jalyn could focus on was the red marks on her essay. There were so many red marks. Jalyn had failed yet again today. She could feel her heart beating in her chest. The sound grew louder until it filled her ears with unrelenting pounding. She felt like she was going to be sick. She was a failure.

Jalyn had failed at writing. Failed at the one thing she enjoyed; the one thing that was easy for her. She could feel the tears threatening to crawl down her face and the emptiness in her stomach rising up from within.

Mrs. Ozark continued to talk, but Jalyn could not hear her over the red marks pounding in her ears. The list of failures started mocking her, "First you woke up late, then Maddie told you no one liked you, then Ethan used you for your homework, now...now your writing sucks. This is too much! This is too much! You are a failure." As the room started to spin, Jalyn muttered quietly to the teacher that she wasn't feeling well, and she needed to go to the nurse.

Not waiting for an answer, Jalyn ran out of the room and went straight for the nearest bathroom. She bent over the toilet desperate to regain some control of what was happening to her. But nothing happened. She realized she had nothing to throw up. She had only eaten half an apple, and she skipped lunch to sell flowers. There was nothing to do. She had no solution. All she could do was grab some toilet paper, hold it over her mouth, and just cry and cry. In between sobs Jalyn heard a quiet voice in the back of her mind.

"I am not enough." Jalyn heard this repeated in the back of her mind. "How could I give every ounce of my effort to everything I do, and it is not enough? I am not enough."

She dragged herself off the floor and went straight to the nurse. She told her that her stomach hurt and she needed to go home. Jalyn never went home sick from school. She had only missed four days in her entire school career, and even that was under protest. She hated missing school, but today was more than she could handle.

Her brother came to pick her up because she was not ready to let her parents see her like this. They would have too many questions that she was not ready to answer. Thank goodness her brother was still home from school. As she got in the car all she could say was, "It's too much. I have no control." As she laid her head on the window, she could feel sleep arrive as she faintly heard her brother say, "Poor girl, you know none of us are really in control, right?"

At home, her brother helped her walk to her bed. She was thankful she hadn't driven to school that day. She was thankful that it was just her and her brother. She fell back asleep with an empty mind... not even thinking about Maddie, or the volleyball game she was missing, or the science test she skipped.

Ethan

After Ethan cooled off in the bathroom, he wandered the hallways until the bell rang for the next period. He wanted nothing more than to avoid homeroom with Maddie.

He successfully avoided her, and pretty much everyone else, for the rest of the day. After school he headed straight to the brook walk, Westwood's name for the popular sidewalk that runs next to the brook in town. He and some guys from school usually met once a week to place bets on some upcoming college football games. It was easier to meet at the park in the woods since no adults could bother them there. It wasn't exactly legal, but it was profitable. Since Ethan ran it, even if he lost his games, he would still get 5% off the top of the total winnings. He had found the perfect group of guys who were suckers for a bet, and not bright enough to care that Ethan took a little bit off the top each time. He cringed knowing he sounded just like his dad, but whatever, sometimes you have to take care of yourself first.

Once the usuals were there Ethan started, "Who do you like for this weekend, guys?" He wrote down their bets while handing out the winnings from last week. "And the rest goes to me. Pleasure doing business with you," Ethan laughed under his breath.

The boys went back and forth for a while. Ethan did not join in on the conversation but instead focused his attention on the brook running beside them. He loved the water and this part of the park especially. When the group finally decided on their bets, Ethan let his focus return to the group where he jotted down their bets and sent them on their way. Once everyone left, Ethan was all alone. The last thing he wanted to do was go home to face his mom who worked so annoyingly hard to be happy and positive all the time for Ethan. He knew she wasn't really happy. Her "niceness" was so aggravating. He much preferred to be by himself or with other miserable people.

As Ethan sat on the bench by the creek, he felt nothing. He liked being out by the flowing water, in the middle of nowhere, with no thoughts in his head, and with no cares of anything in this world. This was his happy place - if you could call Ethan happy. This place had the power to drain Ethan of the strong emotions he had most of the time. Of course, Ethan knew that all it took was one stray thought of his dad, or mom, or life, and he could spiral out of control in a muddy mess of emotions. Unfortunately, this time he let one thought, then another, then another enter his mind. Suddenly, he spiraled into such an angry fit that he took one rock and launched it into the trees, then another, and another until more than an hour had passed. He was left with tears spilling down his face and sweat pouring down his back. Ethan had launched every rock in his path into the depths of the trees around him, but he finally got to a place of nothingness again. He sat back down on the bench, thankful for the emptiness in his mind.

Maddie

Lately, more and more, Maddie had been looking for ways to hide from her life. She dazed off in class, took the long way home after pitching practice, and avoided friends. She knew she couldn't do this forever, but she honestly did not think she had many other options.

On this particular day after pitching practice, she was driving home from practice and instead of stopping for a Slurpee, because, well, she really had no money, she decided to just go sit by the brook walk. That should buy her some time before she had to head home.

As she started down the walk, she took deep breaths trying to get the weight off her chest. A little down the walk she saw a boy about her age sitting on a bench. She looked closely and realized it was Ethan. "Shit!" she shot out. She did not want to run into Ethan on a lonely sidewalk after the way he treated her at that party, but she also knew she couldn't turn around at this point.

Maddie always had an intuitive spirit about her. She seemed to always see the best in people and just seemed to accept people for who they were. She really did not have expectations for those around her. Why would she? She did not want people to have expectations for her. But she was not sure what to make of Ethan sitting on the bench just staring into the brook. He looked so still and focused, like a tourist statue sitting next to the brook waiting for the picture-perfect moment with onlooking walkers.

Maddie could not help herself, as she passed Ethan, she waved him out of his trance and said hello. Up close she could see his tear-stained cheeks and blank expression.

He just looked at her without words. Not known to worry about awkward moments, Maddie sat down without asking permission, and she immediately started talking.

"Ethan, listen. I admit I could have handled the other night much better, but under no circumstances is it okay for you to try and kiss me. I wasn't giving off any signals that I wanted to make out with you. And what you said after, about me being...well, that hurt."

Ethan had a shocked look on his face and looked down. He seemed to shake himself into the moment. "You spit in my face and laughed at me," he paused in a fleeting moment of vulnerability. "How do you think that felt?"

Maddie skipped right past Ethan's feelings, "I know you think you are better than me, better than all of us. You don't always have to look down on everyone. Get over yourself! School is tough on me, and I am stupid -- isn't that the word you used? Do you really need to say it out loud?"

Maddie had said her piece, and now it was time for Ethan to apologize, if he even knew *how*.

"Maddie....what....I don't..." He acted like he was coming out of a trance sleep. The kind of sleep where you wake up and have no idea where you are and what day it is.

"Maddie, you think I think I am better than you? That's the funniest thing I have ever heard," Ethan said sarcastically. "Please, you ignored me in homeroom because you know I don't matter. Not to you or anyone else."

"Wait, what? Ethan, I walked away from you because you were out of line," Maddie jumped up pointing at Ethan. "You owe me an apology! You need to say sorry!"

Ethan looked shocked with his head in his hands. "I was hoping *you* would apologize," he said quietly, drained of emotion. "And besides, I don't think you are stupid. I just said that because you think I am a joke. You laughed at me in front of everyone." He raised his head from his hands and looked right into Maddie's eyes.

"A joke? Ethan, hold up a minute," Maddie could see the desperation in Ethan's eyes, so she sat back down and faced him directly. "I feel like we are having two different conversations. You are cool, almost too cool for the rest of us. We know it, and you know it. People are drawn to you, and you don't need us. Most of the time you seem to have enough confidence for 5 people! Sorry, but it is true!" Maddie stared back at Ethan with a perplexed look on her face.

Ethan was lost in his thoughts and looked at the brook hoping to find some sense in all of this. "No, Maddie, you have it all wrong. I am nothing. Everything knows it. No one cares about me or wants to be a friend, which is fine. I don't need friends. I don't need anyone." Ethan's face was bright red. He had never really opened up to anyone before. This felt too real, too raw. He was incredibly uncomfortable.

"See!" Maddie jumped up, "Right there, you say you don't need friends. We all need friends, Ethan, but you give off this vibe that you don't need us, and it pushes people away. It's okay to let people know you need them. I desperately need my friends. They see me for the real me and accept me as I am. That's gold. I tell them I need them all the time."

"That's because everyone loves you." Maddie couldn't tell if that was sincere or sarcastic, and Ethan's distance stare did not help.

"I don't know about that, but I love them, and I let them know about it. I feel the most real when I am with friends. The rest of the time, it is all pretending. I am no good at school, and the thought of having to go to four more years of school in college makes me feel like I have no future. In fact, I was coming down here to escape going home, to somehow escape my future."

"Me too," Ethan could not believe that the cool, confident Maddie felt insecure and worried. He really hadn't spent much time wondering how other people felt nor did he honestly care how they felt.

Ethan tried to fight off the urge to open up to Maddie, but something inside of him longed to tell someone how he felt. "This is the only place where I can just sit with an empty mind and ignore the emotions inside. I hate, I hate so much. I hate everything and everyone most of the time." Once he started, he couldn't stop, "I hate my dad. I hate my mom for her constant fake niceness. I even hate me, and I hate anyone who thinks I am a joke!" He was out of breath and could feel his face was bright red with embarrassment. "Maddie, I'm sorry about the party. I am sorry."

Neither Maddie nor Ethan knew what to say at that moment. They both came to this spot to escape the world, and they found themselves opening up to the most unlikely person. Both of them felt this, so they sat awkwardly together with their eyes focused on anything but each other.

Finally, Maddie muttered that she should go. Ethan turned to her and asked, "How could your home be so bad?"

Maddie hesitated, "My parents have worked very hard to give me the world with tutors and private coaches. They want me to get a scholarship for softball. We are not exactly in a position to pay for college. It's just, I hate school so much, and it hates me right back. I don't want to let them down, but I have no other options. They need me to go to college, but I know I am not college material."

Ethan was stunned by this confession and his confidence returned. "Seriously? You know that's not actually true, right? There are tons of great jobs out there that don't require some stupid diploma. Most of the people in my family haven't gone to college, and they're doing just fine. Some are more than fine."

Maddie froze. It was as if Ethan was speaking a foreign language she had never heard before. No college? "Yeah, right," but Maddie appreciated this side of Ethan, maybe even liked it. He seemed to have a different perspective than anyone else she knew.

"Ethan, you are not nothing, and you are not a joke. I don't think you realize just how many people would love to be friends with you."

With that, Maddie walked back to her car, rewinding the events of the past hour in her head.

"Not go to college??" The thought was like a bright light in her head of heaviness, and it glowed with so much happiness. It sounded amazing, but it wasn't real life. That's a dream world. Maddie may not be school-smart, but she had a good head on her shoulders, and she knew this was not reality. College was the only ticket to a good future.

CHAPTER 4

Jalyn

Jalyn opened her eyes in a daze, confused where she was and what time it was. The smell of dinner filled her nose as she slept soundly on her bed. She had never felt calmer with a sense of warmth in her heart. This was amazing. She snuggled the pillow for a moment more as she slipped further into her covers.

When she finally stumbled down to dinner, satisfaction filled her heart. As she sat at the table, the reality of the world slowly started to eclipse the contentment she felt. Her parents could see the uneasiness in her eyes, and she could feel the uneasiness in her stomach. They asked her what was wrong. The guilt came pouring in thick, and she explained that she felt bad for missing the volleyball game this afternoon and her science test. In her mind, she could not believe she had let herself go home sick from school. How could she let her team down like that? Would she even have time to make up her test? Suddenly, she had so much more to deal with and take care of, and her to-do list came flooding back into her mind. Her parents said everything would be okay, but she knew they were just covering up their disappointment.

Jalyn quickly finished the rest of her dinner, fully consumed with her own thoughts and worries. As she sat there, her family chatted about work, upcoming events, and interesting stories from their day. Jalyn could barely make out a word of the conversation. All she could think about was how she would never recover from missing so much of her day. She quickly excused herself from the table, ready to get rid of the delicious dinner she just ate. As she sat on the floor poised above the toilet, she was ready to regain control of her life. Downstairs she could hear her grandparents walking in the door. They were stopping by before her brother headed back to school.

As Jalyn sat cross-legged with her head on the toilet, she could hear the muffled sound of conversation below. Eventually, she freshened herself up and came out after her mom knocked on the door to see if she was going to say goodbye. She feigned a smile putting on her costume of composure before she walked downstairs to say goodbye to her grandparents.

Her grandpa asked, as he always did, if she would walk him to his car. Her smile became real and she relaxed. She had come to love these "walks" because she got her grandpa all to herself, and her grandma did not mind staying to chat a little longer inside. He was different from her parents, not in a good or bad way, just different. Her parents were wildly successful and incredibly intelligent, but she loved her grandpa's sense of adventure and aura of ease. Everything he did seemed to be driven by passion and excitement. Even working in the grocery business was still an adventure to him. He had such a zest for life. Jalyn felt she was more like her parents though in their focused, straightforward lifestyle. Everything was a job, and they gave it their all. It really was a wonderful, dependable way to live life.

As Jalyn and Grandpa walked hand-in-hand, they laughed about a story Grandpa told about one of his grocers and a wrong order of banana. As they approached the car, Grandpa asked Jalyn if she was feeling better from school today.

Embarrassed, Jalyn said she was fine and that she was ready to get back to it tomorrow. Grandpa looked down, and Jalyn could tell he was debating a conversation in his head.

"Jalyn, that is what I am afraid of. Do you want to 'get back to it'?"

"Of course, Grandpa! What do you mean?"

"Jalyn, did I ever tell you the story of how I came to this country and started our store?"

"Sure, Grandpa, lots of times."

"You may have heard the storybook version, but I mean the real version?" He could tell by her pause that Jalyn had no idea what he was talking about. "Jalyn, my entire family had been farmers for many generations. When I realized I wanted to come to America and not continue in the family tradition, I had no idea how to tell my parents. They were proud people who worked hard for our family. I owed them everything, but what I wanted for my life was my own thing. I knew my path was different than my family's. Nothing was scarier than having that conversation with my father."

'What did you do, Grandpa? Why not just stay and become a farmer?"

"My grandmother always spoke about inner peace. She would tell me that this peace was a strength, and that it is a gift that every person has inside of themselves. As you know, I am a very religious man, and I realized at a young age that the more of my life that I gave to God, the more of my life that made sense to me. I knew very clearly that my future was moving to America, and once I was here, I became passionate about working with the farmers to help sell their crops. So I guess I did not travel too far from my home. At the end of the day, life is about me and my God first. He guides me where I am supposed to be." He paused, and Jalyn knew the next part was harder for him to talk about. "The problem I see today is that the world is so busy and so loud that people don't take the time to sit quietly and listen to their inner guide, their inner voice. Everyone knows who and what they truly are inside, but so many people are pulled away from their truth by our world. People never spend the time to learn who they are and what they are meant to be. God wants us to be ourselves. He wants us to be the person He created us to be. He loves each and every one of us with all His heart for the true person we are inside. Sometimes we have to face uncomfortable situations to realize our truth. One saying that has always stuck out in my mind is that sometimes in challenging times, it is easier to see the truth through the trees."

Jalyn sat there, not knowing what to say and how this conversation related to her at all. She nodded, taking in the strength of her grandpa. Not only was he physically strong, but he always had an air of contentment and openness about him. Everyone was at ease when Grandpa was around.

"What does that mean? What did you mean about truth and trees?" Jalyn asked.

"I always took it to mean that wintertime is a hard time to live in the forest, but the bare trees give animals a clearer sight into the world around them. For us, when we face darker, harder times it means we may actually be able to see more truth in our lives versus when everything is good." Grandpa could see that Jalyn was deep in thought.

Grandpa rephrased his earlier question to snap Jalyn out of her thoughts. "Jalyn, are you happy?"

"Of course I am, Grandpa." She smiled her perfected smile, but she could feel her Grandpa reading her mind as if it was an open book.

"So you wake up every day and are excited about what you do and who you are becoming?" Grandpa leaned over and put his hands on her shoulders.

Jalyn was utterly stumped. "I mean, I don't know, but that's not the point. I am a kid. I need to work hard now to get to where I want to be. Then I will be happy."

Her grandpa wore a knowing smile. "Oh, I agree that life takes hard work, but it is different when you are working hard on something you are passionate about. It is different if you are working to achieve your dream. What's your dream? To be a pediatrician? Is that what you feel you were meant to be? Is that your dream?"

Jalyn was completely at a loss for words. "Grandpa, I don't know what I am supposed to say? That's what my parents want me to be. I mean, I want it too. I don't know?! I work really hard, and I give everything. ALL THE TIME! What else can I do??" She was working really hard not to get angry at her grandpa.

Grandpa could tell Jalyn was getting upset. "Hunny, no, no, I am not asking you to give more. I am asking you to uncover who you want to be in your heart. You are on the brink of your future, and you are brilliant and capable. I don't want you to follow a different path than the one you were meant to follow. You are too important to this world to do that. This world needs you to be exactly who you were meant to be."

Grandpa smiled and paused; he knew this conversation would not be easy for Jalyn to hear. "The answers to my questions don't come from me...or your parents." Grandpa responded with a glint in his eye. "The answers come from listening to yourself. You have all the answers you need inside of you. Be patient with yourself. You just have to be willing to hear them."

Jalyn was completely flustered by this point. All she did was study and work for the answers - her answers, others' answers, everyone's answers. None of this made sense to her.

Grandpa knew his granddaughter well and understood how much effort she put into life and others. "Jalyn, if you are on the path you were meant to take then the effort won't be work, it will be your heart's passion. No one can stop you from becoming who you were meant to be. No one but yourself." He paused, "Why don't you make a list." This instantly perked Jalyn up. "Make a list and put all the things that make you happy on one side and all the things that don't make you happy on the other side."

"What do you mean? What makes me happy? I don't understand what you want?"

Grandpa just quietly said, "Just try it. And, Jalyn, you know what our last name means, right?"

"Yes, Grandpa. It means God give us direction."

Jalyn's family has always been religious, and Jalyn went to Sunday school and learned everything she was supposed to. Jalyn prayed for family and friends, and asked for forgiveness for her sins. She worked to lead a good Christian life. But the whole idea of having a relationship with God? It was always a little abstract for her. She knew she had to be a good person in order to earn God's love, but her grandpa was talking about something that sounded more selfish.

About her being happy? When did anyone care if Jalyn was happy? Happiness was for little kids picking out their favorite ice cream at the store, not for teenagers deciding on their future.

Grandpa could see Jalyn's internal battle over what he was saying. "Jalyn, I can't tell you what your future will hold. All I can tell you is that if you hand your worries, insecurities, and future over to God, like on a platter," he almost laughed, "God can do amazing things." With that, he kissed her on the forehead and hugged her good night.

So Jalyn went inside -- confused, inspired, sad, feeling various unnamed emotions -- and proceeded to make a list of all the things that made her happy: her schoolwork, her volleyball team, her friends, her family, class officers, her projects. The list went on and on. She did not have anything in the other column.

She thought, "I am a happy person. My life is good. I have nothing in my life that makes me unhappy."

Then, a voice from the back of her mind broke in, "Really?! Seriously?! Jalyn, just think about it. Don't think about other people. Think about you, just you. What makes you happy? Does this list really make you truly happy? Like in your core, happy? Is this your truth? Is it real?"

Jalyn closed her eyes and worked to picture herself in the future working in the medical field. Nothing came to her. She closed her eyes even tighter. Still nothing.

Jalyn had no words, just a pit in her stomach.

She didn't really get what was even going on and why she had to do this? Of course, this list made her happy. She had worked hard to get this list the way it was. Why would she not be happy?

Jalyn had no idea if this was true, but she had no other list, no other happiness. Her grandpa's request seemed like a stupid task.

A week had passed since Grandpa had visited Jalyn, and Jalyn was obsessed with the list she created. She knew that she hadn't gotten the "answer" correct. Clearly, by the conversation she had with her grandpa, she was supposed to have some other answers, but there was no answer key out there. These were the things that made Jalyn happy. It was pretty simple. She was so focused on thinking about the list that Jalyn did not see Ethan heading her way after class. He had texted her the night before asking for her homework answers, and she did not feel like answering. But Ethan was not one to take no for an answer, and he sought her out in-between periods.

"Jalyn, what's up? Did you see my text? Listen, I'll forgive you for not responding as long as you help on some homework I have today." Ethan gave his best win-her-over smile knowing Jalyn would never say no, but Jalyn seemed different today.

"Ok, Ethan, whatever you need." Those were the words she spoke, but Jalyn kept walking forward in a focused daze with no homework being handed over. After Ethan continued to pursue her, she turned and faced him head-on, "Ethan, no. Just no. Go do your own homework, and stop taking my answers! I work hard on homework, and it is not ok for you to come in and just take my hard work away!" Jalyn shouted with her fists held tight.

For a moment the world stopped. No one could believe she had spoken those words, especially Jalyn. She felt so good, but Ethan looked completely shocked, and a little lost. She started to walk away from him and head into class.

Jalyn had gone against every instinct she had, she violated everything she stood for and stood up for herself against Ethan. She expected to feel horrible, but this voice from within was cheering, "Yes! Yes! Yes!"

Before Jalyn could process a thought, she responded, "That felt so good!" with a smile on her face. But as soon as a thought could enter her mind, Jalyn instantly knew that she had made a mistake. "No, I was rude. I should not have done that. Shoot, he is going to be upset with me." The panic spread swiftly to every ounce of her body, and she wanted to run and find Ethan.

Jalyn paused for a moment and wondering what her grandpa would say in this situation, "Jalyn, that felt good because what you said was true. For the first time in a long time, you spoke your truth, and you were right. It felt really good." But Jalyn felt guilty. "You feel guilty, but is it ok for him to take advantage of you? You do all the work, and he uses you to get the answers. Is this a relationship of give and take? Does he help you as much as you help him?" Jalyn knew the answers to her questions.

Jalyn sat there frozen. She knew the simple answer to all of these tough questions, "No."

Jalyn repeated it again louder, "No!!!"

Ethan

"Wow! Holy shit! Jalyn never yells like that." Ethan said to himself as he walked down the hallway burning with embarrassment. First Maddie called him out, now Jalyn.

As he took a moment to breathe, he realized that no one really ever talked to him that way. Almost everyone was afraid of him. He stood there stunned remembering how Jalyn had huffed and walked right past him into class. Out of the corner of his eye, he saw people staring at him, and Jalyn was sitting in class with a big smile on her face. It almost looked as if she was nodding to herself.

Ethan's world was in a spin. Everything seemed to be out of sorts at that moment. Earlier that week he and Maddie "had a moment," and now people were getting the guts to stick up to him in the hallways. He was desperate to understand.

After school that day, he went back to the brook, back to the spot where he felt the calm emptiness. As he sat trying to "quiet" his mind, he became strangely aware of how stupid he looked and felt. In the silence, all he could feel was his anger, his embarrassment, and his sadness rushing over him. There was nothing in this world he hated more than to feel these feelings. He did everything in his power to bury these feelings way down deep. Now here he was bringing them to the surface. How stupid he was to think he mattered. At that moment, all he wanted to do was run away, scream, and punch everything and anything he saw. Just as Ethan was about to storm off, Jalyn showed up walking on the path. "Seriously?!" Ethan thought, "Is there a pamphlet up at school or something about this place!

She kept her distance from the angry Ethan. "What the hell?" Ethan shouted. "Why are you here?"

"Last time I checked, the brook walk was open to everyone!" Jalyn said, uncharacteristically rude. Under her breath she muttered, "There is no place to escape in this town!"

Twice in one day he was yelled at by Jalyn. What is the world coming to?!

As he looked closer at Jalyn, he could see tears welled up in her eyes. He hated to see people crying. "Whoa, hold up. Jalyn, what's wrong?"

Jalyn just started crying. "What do you care? You only care if I give you homework. You don't care about me. I know...I annoy you," she said in her best sarcastic voice. "Believe me, I've been told. What do you want me to do about it? Do you want me to find my own brook to walk by?"

Ethan could tell she was truly asking him a question. "Uhhh, listen, Jalyn, it's fine. Whatever. It's fine."

"No, it's not. You used me to get homework. I work my ass off, and you just expect to walk up and get my hard work. I'm done with all of that. I don't know what that means, but I am done."

Jalyn sat crying. Ethan instinctively put his arm around her. He really had no idea what to do.

"Jalyn, you are right, you probably deserve better than that. I am sorry."

"Probably?" she asked.

"You do deserve better than that," Ethan said plainly.

"They should call this the brook of truth after all of this honesty crap," Ethan said with a laugh. Jalyn looked at him confused. She had no idea what he meant because she did not know about the conversation he and Maddie had at this same spot.

"Ethan, I have no clue what I am doing. I am so lost, and have no idea who I am. I just need you to cut me some slack and not hate me because of today. I can't handle anyone hating me right now," Jalyn cried.

They both sat quietly beside the brook. Eventually, Jalyn started thinking back to a poem from English class.

Out of nowhere, Jalyn spoke, "This reminds me of a poem I once read about a river: 'I told you before, I am a reflection of you. I mirror you what you feel...what you think. I simply help you see the truth within you. I did not create anything that did not already exist in you.'" She paused for a moment, "I feel like it is a poem my grandpa would tell me."

"What does it mean?" Ethan asked.

"I have no idea. Apparently, deep inside, we all know who we are supposed to be in life. It's there. Crystal clear, deep inside. Isn't that nice? I work so hard for everything in my life, and some amazing secret is there just waiting to come out? What the fuck? Oops. Sorry! I never talk like that." Jalyn never really did.

"I know, right! Don't people suck? They piss me off, and that is their fault," Ethan shared.

Jalyn felt like her world was in a tailspin. "Yes, Ethan, people do suck sometimes, but don't be so quick to get pissed off. It's not your fault that other people suck, but you have complete control over your reaction to them. Take responsibility for your own words and actions. No one makes you say the things you say. You decide how you treat others? It doesn't have to be motivated by the actions of others," Jalyn had no idea where these words came from but went on to challenge Ethan just like her grandpa had challenged her. "I challenge you that instead of getting angry at other people, instead, try to learn two new things about the people in your life. Don't instantly push them away with your anger. Switch the focus and learn two new things about their life."

Ethan was at a loss with this challenge. He wanted so badly to say something rude to Jalyn, but that is exactly what she said not to do. He was not into all this closeness and getting-to-know-you nonsense. He didn't do relationships, he preferred people from a distance. Instead of saying something, he just walked away in silence. He did not know what to say or do. For the first time, in a long time, someone had put him in his place. He paused and realized this was actually the second time today this had happened.

As Ethan drove home, he felt numb. Did he really always respond with anger? Was it his fault or the way he reacted to others that made people so afraid of him? He seriously always thought something was wrong with the rest of the world. It never occurred to him that something might have been wrong with *him* all along. As he pulled into his driveway, he just wanted to sit on his porch, not quite ready to go inside.

After some time passed, his mom stuck her head out of the door. "Ethan, are you ok? I made dinner. You hungry?" she asked.

Ethan noticed at that moment that his mom kept her distance from him and did not come fully onto the porch. He got a sickening pit in his stomach, and this made him mad. Why was his mom always making him so mad, making him feel so horrible this way? Just as he was about to yell at her, he remembered what Jalyn had said, and he took a deep breath instead, and said, "Mom, will you come sit by me?" Ethan could see the hesitation in her eyes and body movement, and he felt it in his heart.

"Um, sure, I mean, yes, of course," his mom responded. His mom quickly took a seat next to him. Neither of them knew what to say next.

All Ethan could focus on was what Jalyn had told him to do. He needed to learn two new things about his mom. "So, Mom, I know you and my dad divorced when I was two, but I don't know why you divorced. Whenever I asked when I was little, you seemed to give me a vague answer. Eventually, I stopped asking. Is that something you can tell me?" Ethan couldn't believe he was asking such a serious question. He had never had an in-depth conversation with his mom before. But it truly was a question he wanted to know.

"Oh, Ethan, that was so long ago. Who remembers what exactly happened?" He could see his mom's eyes looking off into the distance, but he figured it might be the way-distant past she was trying to see. Ethan could feel the anger coming back into his stomach and crawling up his neck. He should never have listened to that girl. This was stupid. Here he was trying to learn something about his mom, and she was being her usual dismissive self. In spite of his anger, he persisted.

"Mom, I am trying to learn something about you. Can you help me out here?!" His anger threatened to come out, but he swallowed hard to contain it.

His mom looked out into the yard for a good five minutes before speaking. "Ethan, it's complicated. My marriage to your dad was not good. I don't think it is worth talking about." Ethan could see her pulling away at the napkin in her hand.

Despite the sadness in her eyes, Ethan could not turn back now. "You never talk about anything. You don't care about me. You bury everything inside, and you are just a shell of a person. What am I supposed to learn from you? How do you live with yourself?" Ethan could feel the heat in his cheeks and his heartbeat pounding in his chest. All of this started out as a simple question, but now he realized he needed to know this. He was not sure why, but somehow it seemed like the most important question in the world right now. He hated that his mom wasn't talking to him. Ethan could see his mom felt the same way because her face was as red as his right now.

"Shut up! Shut up! Shut up! You have no idea what you are talking about!" his mom had never talked to Ethan that way. Her anger stopped him in his tracks. He froze and waited for her to continue. Suddenly, the words poured from his mom's mouth like water, "Your father is an evil man. He was awful, awful to me. He was physically and mentally abusive. He used everyone in his life for his own gain. No one mattered unless they benefited him. His charm fooled me for a very long time. It wasn't until he went to go hit you one night because you kept crying and crying. Well, that was the night I knew I couldn't live this life anymore. I jumped in front of him and stopped him. He put me in the hospital, and your aunt came and helped me figure out a plan to leave him. We both left him that night, you and me, so he couldn't hurt either of us again. And he has never hurt you or me since that day, but he is still a lying scumbag of a person. Always has been, and I imagine he always will be."

Ethan sat there unable to process what he just heard. He looked at his mom, and for the first time ever, he saw a strong person with conviction in her heart and decisiveness on her lips. He had never seen this side of his mom. Or was it always there and he just refused to see it?

"Why didn't you tell me this before?" Ethan was stunned at how this conversation had gone.

"How do you tell a little kid that story?" his mom asked. "Your father barely shows up as it is. That alone is hard enough on a little kid. You never needed to know the full story. Then it became an old story, and I didn't want to relive the past. We have our own life together, and your father only comes around every once in a while. He is always gone as fast as he comes."

Ethan sat processing all of this for a long time. Finally, he spoke, "I am sorry that happened to you. You were brave to protect us like that." Even as the words came off of his lips, Ethan couldn't believe they were coming from his mouth. He felt so raw, so vulnerable. Almost kid-like. What an awful feeling!

His mom wiped tears from her eyes, and sensing Ethan's discomfort, she said, "Well, it's all ancient history anyway."

At that moment, Ethan realized he had only learned one new thing about his mom, so he pushed his luck to ask one more question. "Mom, what do you like best about your life right now?"

"Ethan, I love you, and our house, and my job. Our life makes me happy."

Now it was Ethan's turn to have tears coming to his eyes. He couldn't remember the last time he cried, but as soon as he tried to get words out, tears poured out with them. "But, Mom, I am so mean to you."

Ethan's mom came over to hug him right away, and paused, carefully selecting her words, "There is a lot of anger inside of you, Ethan. You have every right to have anger. It's true, it's hard to have you be so angry towards me, but I'm the safe person in your life. I pray every day that you find a way to overcome your anger and begin to live the life I know you were meant to live."

His mom kissed his head and went inside. Just as she was about to close the door, she yelled out, "There is meatloaf in the frig when you are ready for dinner."

Ethan just sat on the porch in awe of the day he had. Everything was ass-backwards, and this sent Ethan into a spin. Everything he was certain of this morning was up for grabs right now - his mom, his life, his thoughts. Everything Jalyn said now seemed right. But how could some random goody-good know so much about his life? Ugh! There it was again. He was being mean. His mind drifted to Jalyn from earlier that day. How did this goody-goody, people-pleasure suddenly get the guts to stick up to him? I mean, come on - how did she know I wouldn't respond in a bad way? His anger liked to get the best of him. But she was right. Wasn't she? Ethan was using her. It wasn't her job to do his homework. What about Hannah? It wasn't her job either...

All of this reality was taking its toll on him. Ethan headed straight to bed without eating. His world was like a snow globe that was just shook up, and the pieces were all up in the air. He had no idea where they would all land, but he knew this whole "learn two things about the people in your life" seemed to make things better with his mom. Maybe he will try it with someone else tomorrow.

Maddie

She had been hanging on to her life by a thread, and it wasn't even her own thread. It was the thread her parents, and tutors, and coaches had woven for her. Nothing about her life was hers. She required support in all aspects of what she did. Take away the supports and you take away her existence. Maybe she shouldn't exist.

Ethan offered an alternative, a different version of her life, or at least the idea that she could find a way to exist on her own two feet in a way she knew she was capable of doing.

Maddie's thoughts were interrupted by her mom asking her to pass the potatoes. Her dad was diving into his usual routine of discussing next week's game plan. Our plan to conquer the world, my world, as they saw it. As my dad was analyzing the best college pitchers for next season, I burst into tears. All I could think was...all I could say was, "It's too much. It's too much." At that moment, everyone froze and looked at me.

"Maddie, what's wrong? All we want is what's best for you. If this week's tutoring is too much, we can have them skip tomorrow. We can give you a break. I know it has been a lot lately with coaching, tutoring, and school, but we figured since it was junior year, this is the time to make your dreams come true," Dad said.

Maddie couldn't think. It was all too much. She left without saying a word and went straight to her room and locked the door. She wanted to disappear or have a drink or a hit or something. Anything to escape the pressure. Her chest felt like it would squeeze shut. It was so heavy, too heavy. Maddie started to see the room spin and everything went black.

She woke up to her mom and dad over her. "Maddie, Maddie. Wake up. Maddie, are you okay?"

Maddie felt woozy and could barely talk.

"Maybe we should call an ambulance," her dad said.

"Hold on. I think maybe she just had a panic attack," Mom said. "Maddie, just take three deep breaths. Tell me one thing you can see."

"Your face," Maddie muttered.

"Tell me one thing you can touch?" asked mom.

"My bed," Maddie felt the ruffle under her hand.

"Tell me one thing you can hear," Mom pressed on.

"Your voice," she answered, starting to feel a little better. Life started to come back to Maddie's body, and everything came back into focus.

"I think you are going to be ok," her mom hugged her.

Both of Maddie's parents enveloped her in a massive hug as she whispered, "I can't breathe!"

"Oh, sorry," her parents said, barely letting go of their grip on their daughter. "You went upstairs and we heard this loud bang. Dad opened the door, and you had fainted on the floor. We love you so much. Maddie, talk to us. What's going on? You're freaking us out a bit here."

Maddie, still weak, thought about it for a minute, and finally said, "You won't want to hear what I have to say."

"All that matters right now is what you have to say. Hunny, you just fainted. Something must be going on. You have to tell us," her mom begged.

"I...I don't know...it is all just too much lately. There is this pressure on my chest, this 800-pound weight right here, and I hate it. I hate it." Maddie started to cry. Her truth poured out of her eyes and her mouth.

"Maddie, help us understand what you are saying," Dad asked.

"Everything is too much: school, softball, college, your expectations, everything. I can't do it all. I am not the person you want me to be. I wish I was, but I am not," Maddie felt the pressure leaving her, but it was being replaced with nerves. What would her parents say? What would they think of her?

"Whoa, Maddie, what do you mean? What are you saying? All you have ever wanted was to pitch and play softball in college. It's your dream. We have sacrificed so much to help you achieve your dream." her dad looked heartbroken. Her parents looked at her with sadness in their eyes.

Maddie realized all of this was true. It was her dream, and her parents had sacrificed everything to help her. Maddie just sobbed and sobbed. Her parents sat holding her - not speaking, just being there until she finally said, "I love softball, but not like this. I hate school. I am terrible at it. The tutors get me through. Me saying 'thank you, thank you, thank you' to everyone has helped me inch my way through, but that is no way to live. I love softball, but the thought of having to go through four more years of school in college...well, I feel like I am trapped in a cage, and I would do anything to escape. And I mean anything!" Maddie fell backward with exhaustion. She had told her truth, and she was exhausted.

She knew she had rocked her parent's world. They were both looking at each other, desperate for the other one to say something.

Finally, her mom broke in, "Maddie, we just want you to be happy."

Her dad was still struggling with all of this news, and mom shot him a glance. "We are on your team. All we ever wanted was to help make your dreams come true. A college degree is something that will make your future better. You will always have that to fall back on. Who cares if it takes tutors to get you through? Your mom and I struggle for everything we have, and we wanted better for you."

She could see the give and take between her parents, "But, we never wanted you to feel like you were trapped. We had no idea you felt this way. We would never want that for you. We did not realize that everything was pushing you to the point of breaking. That's no way to live."

It was dad's turn. "Maddie, let's take some time to think about this. You don't have to be dramatic. There is always a solution. Let's discuss what you want and what's best for your future? Like your mother said, we are on your team, but this is just temporary. Stay the course and you will be fine."

Her parents looked at each other, and Maddie broke down in tears again. She should just listen to her dad. He was right. There was no reason to be so dramatic. She felt like the worst daughter, and she knew this would not be the last time her parents discussed this with her. They were set on her getting a degree.

"I am letting you down. I know how much money you pay for all my tutors and coaches. I can't just throw that away. I don't want to throw that away. All your money spent would be for nothing," Maddie said desperately.

Dad took a deep breath, "Maddie, we have worked hard to give you more than what we had. We may not have a ton of money, but we are happy. We want you to have a chance to find your happiness in life. Getting a degree will make that easier for you. You have to go to college. Let your mother and I talk about this and you rest."

Maddie's heart was a mix of guilt and pressure, but she could not ignore the truth inside.

"Mom and Dad, I am thankful for all you have done for me. I really am, but the reality is that I am terrible at school. I can barely imagine getting through the next two years, let alone four years after that. That thought alone makes my chest feel tight. If I could play college softball and not have to go to school, I would do that in a heartbeat. If I could skip the class part, then I would be all in," Maddie explained.

"That's why we pay to get you tutors," her dad blurred out but stopped once her mom shot him a look. "Rest now, and we will figure this out. In the end, we will find the right solution," Dad said, sounding fairly convincing.

Her mom squeezed Maddie's hand, as Maddie said, "I don't know what to do?" It was the only response that was true and real. "I don't know yet."

"You are a bright light in this world, Maddie. Take time to think it through. We can help you sort this out. For now, let's cancel your pitching coach for the next few weeks and go from there. Can we agree to keep your school tutors because, let's be honest, no matter what you do, you will need to graduate high school," Mom said.

"Yes," Maddie replied. "Can I please sleep now?" she asked her parents.

"Yes, of course," they said and kissed her head as they left.

Maddie felt both relieved and terrified with the world she had just created. She took three deep breaths and just cleared her mind. She had told her truth, and her parents heard her. There is nothing better than to be heard and seen. However, she had no idea what she wanted to do with her life. Who knows what the future would hold, certainly Maddie had no clue.

Just as she was about to fall asleep, her mom opened the door, "Maddie, do you want to know something? Every single human being has a superpower. This is something they do better than anyone else," she explained.

"Well, if you were paying attention, Mom, school is NOT one of my superpowers. Nothing about school is a superpower for me," Maddie confided.

"School does not measure all superpowers, Maddie. There are plenty of superpowers that make you a success in life, but schools do not teach everything you need to know about life."

"I'm so confused," Maddie said.

"Some people have an amazing heart. They are meant to help others in need. Some people are good with their hands. These people can build masterpieces out of wood or metal or other materials. All these skills might not be measured in school, but these are certainly skills that the world needs."

"Mom, then what is my superpower?"

"Well, that's one question you do not need a tutor to help you answer," Mom said with a knowing smile.

"I clearly need help because I have no idea what you are talking about," Just then, Maddie's eyes closed from the exhaustion of the day. Mom smiled and whispered in Maddie's ear, "You will, Maddie. You will."

As the light faded so did Maddie's consciousness, and she fell into a deep sleep.

CHAPTER 5

Jalyn

Jalyn could not shake the situation with Ethan or the list her grandpa had asked her to make. She spent a lot of time thinking about it and overthinking it the next few days.

No, it wasn't okay for Ethan to steal her homework, but what was she supposed to do? People liked her because she always knew the answer. People liked her because she could help them out or fix their problems. People liked her because she worked harder than anyone else. Her team liked her because she could serve a mean jump serve. Her teachers liked her because she always had the right answer. Her friends liked her because she always had a great idea for a fundraiser or event. She realized that she made people happy by making their lives easier and solving their problems. If she changed these roles, then no one would like her, right?

Ethan needed her because she helped him, and if she stopped helping him then he wouldn't like her anymore. She made a mental list of things she would say the next time she saw Ethan. One way or another, she would make things better.

"Good, at least things feel back to normal," she said to herself after her fourth attempt that day to purge her way back into control. "Now, I need to work through my notes for class so I can be 100% ready." She snapped herself back into her normal routine.

After school, Jalyn was walking to her volleyball locker when Ethan popped out of nowhere.

"Jalyn, we need to talk," Ethan said.

"I agree, Ethan. Listen, I'm sorry. I wasn't feeling well the other day, and I would have never normally acted that way. I will help you whenever you need. Afterall, that's what I am here for, right?" Jalyn had been waiting to let these words escape and put things back to normal.

Ethan barely registered what Jalyn had said. He seemed like he was a million miles away. "Jalyn, what do you like best about school?" That was one thing. He still needed to ask another question later.

"Ummm, huh?" Jalyn was not expecting this response from Ethan.

"You heard me. What do you like best about school?"

"I guess the classes. I love learning. I especially love writing in my English class," Jalyn never expected that he would work to learn something about her! This made her blush. She hoped she answered him correctly. This was odd behavior, even for Ethan.

"Okay, second question, why do you help me?" Ethan asked, truly wanting to know the answer.

Jalyn tripped over her answer. She couldn't help but notice the piece of hair that hung over his bright brown eyes. She searched her brain for what to say and before she could decide she blurted out, "Because I like when you pay attention to me." She was shocked by the honesty of her words, so she backed away towards the girls' locker room as fast as she could. "I...I have to go."

She couldn't help but smile when she went into the locker room. Smile and smack herself for saying that to Ethan, "Did that really happen?!" She had to shake it off because they were supposed to be on the court in 5 minutes. She looked at herself in the mirror, and said, "Ok, time to focus!"

Dinner that night was not the usual praise-session Jalyn was used to. "It is such a shame that your team lost to the Chargers that night you went home sick. Now your team is one win short of taking first in conference. Did you make up all your work from when you were sick?" her mom jumped from one topic to another.

The awareness of Jalyn's weakness created a thick layer of guilt that covered her from head to toe. While she knew it wasn't her fault that the team lost, she knew they would have had better odds if she had been there. All she could focus on was what she could do to make her parents happy and her teammates happy. There had to be a way to do this.

As soon as dinner was done, Jalyn went upstairs to focus on studying for tomorrow and finishing some items on her to-do list. But she felt uneasy, something wasn't right. She knew what she had to do. She had to use her tool to get rid of dinner and feel better again. That would give her the sense of control she wanted so badly. The sense of control to fix things from when she was sick and make it up to those around her. At that moment she heard a faint voice in the back of her mind. Usually Jalyn could ignore this voice but lately she was having a harder time. All she wanted to do was focus on her goals and to-do list. Honestly, there was no time for anything else, especially a questioning voice inside of her. But she thought back to what her grandpa had said. She lowered her head and started talking to God about everything that was in her heart.

At school the next day, Ethan tried to talk to her multiple times, but Jalyn was able to dodge him in the hallway. "I just want it to go back to the way it was before. He asks for homework. I give it to him. Done," Jalyn said to herself. "What else could he possibly want from her? She had nothing else he could 'use'. She had nothing else to give."

Finally he cornered her outside of English class. "Jalyn, can we talk?" he asked.

"Ummm, I have to get into class." She had almost made it into the classroom and into the clear, but Ethan was persistent.

Ethan half yelled into the classroom to get her attention. "I owe you an apology." Jalyn felt bad for him since almost everyone in her English class was now looking at him. She grabbed his arm and pulled him into the hallway before he had a chance to embarrassed himself, or her, again. He continued, "You...I should have not asked you to always give me your homework. You are worth more than that." He paused and looked quite nervous, anxiously awaiting her response. Even he was surprised by the words that were coming out of his mouth.

"Ethan, it's fine. Whatever. No big deal. Let's just drop it. Like I said before, I am fine helping you." She hoped that this would just end this nonsense, and then things would go back to normal, but no such luck.

"Would you want to hang out sometime? We could maybe go for a walk down by the Westwood brook....on purpose this time." Ethan gave her a look that all but begged her to say yes. Jalyn could tell this was new territory for him. So, of course, she said yes; she wouldn't want to upset him.

As soon as she left, she smacked her hand against her forehead. What did she just agree to?! Ethan, the most volatile person at Westwood High and she was going to meet him alone...again...by the brook! Wow! Her need to people-please was at an all-time high right now. At least she hadn't committed to a certain day, so she was sure she could squirm her way out of the plans.

The bell rang, and she rushed in English class pleasantly unaware of the memory of the last time she was in this class. That bliss lasted about two seconds because she could see that Mrs. Ozark was still conferencing with students. How could she face that horrific, red-lined English paper again? Red lines meant failure. Period. She couldn't recover from a bad grade in English class. Just as Jalyn was starting to spiral around the idea of being a failure, Mrs. Ozark called her up to her desk.

"I was sorry to see you were sick the other day, Jalyn. I was so looking forward to meeting with you about your narrative writing."

Before the teacher could go on, Jalyn interrupted her, "Mrs. Ozark, I am so sorry. I can see all the mistakes on my paper. It's terrible. Please let me rewrite this. I know I can do better," Jalyn pleaded with her. "I won't let you down. Please, I can't fail...I mean, I can do better."

Mrs. Ozark looked confused. "Jalyn, oh my. Let's start over. I wanted to meet with you because your story was amazing. Your characters were so real and believable. This is a great story. You are a talented writer."

"But all the red marks..." Jalyn just looked at the paper in complete disarray.

"Well, welcome to the world of being a writer. People will always find ways to change or improve your writing based on their style and ideas. Red lines do not mean your paper isn't good. It just means someone else sees a way to leave their mark on your story in hopes of making it better. It is kind of hard to get used to but the world of writing is not black and white. It is all gray," Mrs. Ozark laughed. "But I am getting off topic. The reason I added so many edits to your paper is because I think this story is good enough to enter into the Stenitzer National Writing Awards competition. I wanted to give you my insight to help you. Of course, it is your story, so you can choose to keep my ideas or take them out."

Jalyn had been holding her breath the whole time Mrs. Ozark talked, and her heart was beating so fast in her chest. This was maybe the best compliment Jalyn had ever gotten, but it came with some imperfections.

"Mrs. Ozark, I have no idea what to say. Thank you. I was so worried about being wrong. But you liked my story? National Awards? I have no idea what to say?" Jalyn stuttered.

Mrs. Ozark gave her a knowing smile and put her hand on Jalyn's arm, "Jalyn, I know. Your reputation precedes you. Other classes are different in that you can give the perfect, straightforward answer to the teacher's question. But writing is a little different. I wasn't quite sure how you were going to handle my feedback, but I don't come across writers like you every day. You have a talent, a gift. You could make a living as a writer, you know. Good writers always have a story to tell. Do you have a story to tell?"

Jalyn paused. The abstractness of her question combined with the complete absence of a right answer made Jalyn uncomfortable. "So should I make the changes you suggested and resubmit the paper to you?"

"Yes. You can do that, Jalyn, but please consider submitting it to the competition. I think, with some editing, you could have a real winner here. What do you say?" Mrs. Ozark asked.

"Of course," Jalyn said yes because, let's be real, when does she ever say no?

Ready for some sense of normalcy, Jalyn welcomed the usual ritual of teacher questions and her perfectly-poised answers. By now, Jalyn did not even notice the dirty looks her classmates gave her when she always had the right answers. None of that mattered. All that mattered was she was back to normal.

After arriving home after a tough workout at volleyball, Jalyn plopped herself on the bed, ready for a shower. She looked at her phone and noticed that Ethan had texted her. "Can you meet me at 6 tonight?" Crap! It was 5:45 p.m., and she did not want to go. She thought for a minute on how to get out of this, but finally realized that if she showered quickly, she could probably be at the brook by 6:05 p.m. So she texted back, "Yes, but it may be closer to 6:10."

Once Jalyn arrived down by the brook, she looked around to find Ethan and saw him sitting on the same bench as last time. His brown hair reflected the setting sunlight and his face seemed uplifted, almost happy. As if Jalyn needed a reminder of Ethan's good looks, he looked even more handsome right now.

Jalyn brushed aside her thoughts and walked over to Ethan, ready to get this over with.

Ethan

Ethan was talking to himself again. "Take a deep breath. Be yourself. All you want to do is talk with her as a person and apologize for using her before. Ugh! She was always nice to me, even when I didn't deserve it. Remember what she said, just focus on learning about her." This softness surprised Ethan.

Just then, Ethan saw movement out of the corner of his eye. He realized it was Jalyn and his heart skipped a beat.

Ethan got up to walk toward Jalyn, "Hey, babe, thanks for coming." Ethan added his charming smile to the mix. A voice inside of him screamed, "Ugh! No. That's crap. That's not real! Be real!"

Ethan immediately changed his approach. "Hi, Jalyn, thanks for coming. Have a seat."

"I am not sure why you asked me here. I will still give you my homework, okay? Are we good now?" Jalyn asked with obviously no interest in staying.

"No!" Ethan shouted, but quickly tried to calm himself. "I mean, no. That's not why I asked you here." He took a moment to compose himself. "Listen, I know I am...rough. You have always been nice to me, and I honestly know I probably did not deserve it. But I wanted to show you I can be nice, and I wanted to say sorry. I don't know. I just wanted to show you who I really am."

Ethan looked down at his shoes, then up in the air. He did not know what to say. Maybe someone would appear and just fix all of this. Of course it was just Ethan and Jalyn, and he was up next to talk.

"I don't know the last time I was happy," Ethan said barely over a whisper. He looked like a little kid in that moment with his brown hair hanging down over his eyes.

Jalyn, desperate to figure out the right answer to the situation, said, "Let's be real, Ethan. Who is happy? Aren't we all happy enough? Life is what it is. We go to school, do homework, and live our life. That's a good thing. Why are we even talking about being happy? Who has time to worry about that?" She put her hand gently on top of his and felt a wave of nervousness through her body.

Ethan could feel Jalyn's soft hand on top of his. This closeness gave Ethan an idea and his eyes lit up. He grabbed Jalyn's hand and told her to come with him. He wasn't sure how to make himself happy, but he knew a place that always made him feel better or at least made him as happy as he could be.

He dragged Jalyn through the woods on a never-ending path of pebbles, branches, and directional signs. As Ethan walked, he looked at Jalyn, who looked half intrigued and half scared. He couldn't blame her. This was not really the typical Ethan and this was the first time they had spent any length of time together. After about 10 minutes, Ethan slowed his pace and stopped to catch his breath. Ethan had a glow about him that even Jalyn noticed. He looked and felt happy and alive. He was so nervous to show Jalyn the small pond he had found walking through the woods one day. As he bent down to wipe the wall of branches away, he revealed the beautiful field of flowers and still pond waiting ahead for them. As soon as he walked into the field, he could feel the calm set in. There were butterflies everywhere with an array of flowers and scents in the air. It was like opening the door into a different world. Here he could forget everything about his father, about his life, and just take a break for a moment. He suddenly became aware of Jalyn again, and he felt a mixture of excitement and hesitation. How would she feel about all this? Looking at her face, he knew she was just as much in awe of the scene as he was. He smiled and led her closer to the pond. Jalyn walked slowly around taking in the beauty and softness of each moment. Eventually, Jalyn just sat down, right there in the middle of the flowers. Ethan walked over to her with a genuine smile on his face.

"What do you think?" Ethan asked.

"Ethan, this place is amazing. I feel swept away by all the flowers, butterflies, and that pond. There is not even a tiny ripple in it. It's so calm here," Jalyn looked down with tears in her eyes.

The two of them sat soaking up the field for a while. Ethan could feel the calm setting in. Just then, he noticed Jalyn looking down.

"What's wrong?" Ethan's heart began to race. What could possibly be wrong? All he had done was show her this place. He hadn't said a word. "Jalyn, I didn't mean to upset you." It came out more as a question than a statement.

"You didn't upset me. I am not sure why I am crying. I am not sad at all. In fact, this place is wonderful. I am just a mess, I guess," Jalyn had no other way to explain her reaction. "It's just, you mentioned about being happy, I have been focusing on that lately...you see, my grandpa...and then we came here and I feel so calm, so relaxed. I don't know. The feeling caught me off guard. I pride myself on being on top of everything in my life, being in control of my own success...and emotions. I don't usually have quiet time or take time to just do nothing. For some reason, I feel emotional from the calm. Does that even make sense?"

Ethan really did know what she meant, all too well. Emotions definitely get the best of him quite often.

"Maybe I am not happy, Ethan? Maybe being good at school and being successful at sports and activities isn't making me happy. Gosh, listen to me. What am I even saying? I work so hard for all that. How can I not be happy? All of that should make me feel happy?"

"Jalyn, I know what you are saying. This happiness thing is new to me too. I hated pretty much everyone and everything... that is until recently," he laughed in spite of the seriousness of their conversation. "But listening to you and my mom has made me not feel so much, so much hate, I guess." He paused before deciding whether he would carry on, "I hate myself too. I couldn't even look at myself in the mirror without feeling so much hatred for everything. Then you come along and a simple thing like learning about the people around me seemed to change this feeling inside of me. I don't know what this all is either, but it feels better than before."

"Ethan, I keep ignoring the things my grandpa said to me about happiness. I don't want anything to change, or maybe I do want it to change. My mind is a mess," she paused. "I'm afraid. If I change then people won't like me. Everyone likes me for the things I do and how hard I work. If I stop doing those things, then they will stop liking me. Then where will I be?" Jalyn asked, and Ethan figured she really did not want an answer to that question. "Ethan, you asked me why I always help you. The truth is I figured you would not like me unless I helped you."

Ethan looked into Jalyn's eyes and looked down. He honestly did not know how he would have responded if she stopped helping him, but he wanted to be different now.

Ethan just whispered, "I'm sorry," and he meant it.

They just sat there back-to-back watching nature around them. The minutes blended together, and in that moment they both felt a sense of peace.

Jalyn started to smile. "My grandpa said that if I handed my questions and struggles over to God then he would help guide me with the answers. Suddenly I do that, and I am here with you in the peaceful field. Grandpa said that my true path would be peaceful and not so much struggle. He wants me to find something that I am passionate about."

Ethan was out of his realm. "My family has never been religious. I don't know much about religion."

Jalyn laughed. "I know everything about my religion, but this is the first time I maybe get what my grandpa was talking about when he mentioned his relationship with God or at least I am trying to understand."

"I don't know if God even knows I exist," Ethan continued.

Ethan frowned, and Jalyn realized this was beyond what he was ready for.

"Ethan, my grandfather has always talked to me about his relationship with God. He talks about Him like He is his friend. I never understood that. I understood the religious rules and the responsibilities that I had to be a good person, but I never truly understood what it meant to have a personal relationship with God. I don't know if I fully understand it yet, but I am working on it. Think about it this way, Ethan, you come here to find calm, right? Emptiness as you say. Well, what if what you are calling emptiness is actually peace? Maybe nature is how you feel God. God allows us to connect to him in many ways. You may find your spiritual connection through nature."

Jalyn paused, then continued, "You need to allow the world to guide you. That is the only way to get help. You can't do this on your own. None of us can. Is any of this making sense?"

All Ethan could say was, "I don't know."

"Ethan, out here you seem happier. You have a glow about you. My grandpa talked about finding the real me, the real path. I have no idea what he means but out here it feels a little closer. Do you feel that at all?

This shocked Ethan. He had no idea Jalyn was paying that much attention to him. "Maybe?"

Ethan and Jalyn sat in silence for a long time, each just enjoying the silence and presence of the other person. Little did they know that they each had something that the other needed in order to find their true path, and they would be spending a lot more time together in the future.

Ethan looked at Jalyn, who was already looking back at him. What was Jalyn thinking right now? He imagined that Jalyn was asking herself the exact same question. As this experience faded into the air, the two of them just sat, soaking up the surroundings.

It was Jalyn who broke the silence, "Ethan, I need to go home and study." Ethan nodded and they headed back down the path. Back to their lives.

As Jalyn turned toward her car, Ethan asked, "Can we meet here again?"

Jalyn just nodded and smiled to herself.

Ethan went home that evening with a touch of hope in his heart. And after dinner, he went over to his mom, hugged her, and said, "Thank you."

Later that night before Ethan went to bed, he looked in the mirror and smiled back at his reflection. This was the first time he had smiled at himself in a very long time.

Maddie

Superpower? The only superpower Maddie could think that she had was her pitching. And she knew that there was no future in softball for her. She couldn't be a pitcher for the rest of her life. She was completely stumped by what her mom had said to her. If everyone had a superpower...well...it must be everyone but her. She was used to not measuring up to others in school, so the thought that she was missing a superpower too, well, that seemed about right.

Thank goodness it was the weekend! No more tough questions, no more homework! Just time with friends and freedom. Her escape. She had to admit that her life was not as stressful as before. Her parents had let up a little bit. Probably because they were afraid their anxiety-ridden daughter would return and lose her mind again. Truth be told, Maddie was afraid of that too. She hated the pressure she felt on her insides. So when Maddie asked to spend the weekend at a friend Amelia's house, her parents gladly agreed. They, of course, did not know that Amelia's parents were out of town for a business trip with her mom's job, but they really did not need to know that particular detail.

The evening's festivities began with the usual shotgun beer, followed by lots of laughter and fun. Maddie was jumping from group to group enjoying the conversation, watching a group of girls gossiping about the couple in the corner and some boys were playing beer pong, cheering loudly when their team won. After a little while of chatting with friends and snacking on food in the kitchen, her mind came back to the superpower question. She found herself zoning out of conversations and struggling to stay in the moment. She tried to shake it off but just couldn't. It may have been the drinks, but Maddie started telling a few people what her mom had said and about the idea of everyone having a superpower. Being the good friends that they were, they could see Maddie was looking for their insight on her superpower, and they were very quick to answer her, which surprised Maddie. Amelia had said, "Maddie, you are kidding right? You are the most amazing person I know. You talk to everyone, and you really care about us. I feel so good when I am with you. I know I can trust you, and you always make me smile. Remember when Josh broke up with me. You sat with me while I cried and binge-watched TV until I started to feel better. You made me the most amazing cupcakes. I am not sure anyone else would have done that. If that's not a superpower, then I don't know what is," Amelia answered a stunned Maddie. "You connect with people better than anyone I know, and you are genuine. That is a rare trait these days." Amelia finished and accidentally ran into a boy on the football team spilling her drink on the floor. Amelia quickly went to clean it up, and the two of them started up a conversation as the boy helped her clean up the spill. Maddie used this opportunity to sneak out the front door to the porch.

She enjoyed being with her friends and talking with others, but she had never really thought of being there for others as a superpower. She hadn't realized how much it meant to them. She had only known the happiness it brought her to help others and hear their stories. It was easy. Being friendly was something that always came naturally to Maddie. She sat on the swing and just absorbed the thoughts that came into her head. Finally, Maddie just whispered to herself, "Can my superpower be that I connect well with other people? That I care about them? That seems too easy."

Maddie knew the answer, for the first time in a long time, "Yes, 100%, yes! And that is my superpower."

Maddie continued to talk to herself, "Ok, so what does that mean? Am I supposed to go around being a professional 'friend' my whole life? How does this help me with school...and softball...and my future?" Maddie was back to feeling confused. She laughed, "I guess that is the million-dollar question. Maybe someday I'll figure out the answer. I just need to stay true to myself, and I will know the path to take." She hiccupped and knew that she had enough to drink for the night.

Maddie must have fallen asleep on the swing because she woke up to a friend bringing her inside to sleep on the couch. When she woke up the next morning, she looked around at her friends all over the place and smiled. She thought of the week ahead, and for the first time, she did not feel the weight on her chest. She felt content and focused. She had no idea what she was focusing on, but she knew it had something to do with her superpower.

CHAPTER 6

Jalyn

That afternoon with Ethan will be forever embedded into Jalyn's mind. Things seemed different but were they *really*? She had stuck up for herself with Ethan, and instead of him hating her, they seemed to start a bit of a friendship. She couldn't believe she told Ethan about her grandpa and God. She was not a very religious person, and she is pretty sure she never had a conversation with anyone her age about God before.

Everything Jalyn was feeling made no sense to her, and she was uncomfortable with this feeling. She was actually hoping not to see Ethan again soon. Deep down she figured he was probably using her just like he always had. She had enjoyed being with him, but that was a fluke. She had more important things to focus on now.

Jalyn really did not know how to change her world so that she could find this happiness. That idea seemed frivolous given that she thought she was already plenty happy; she has a good life, good friends, and a good family. It seemed impractical and immature, and frankly a little ridiculous, to work for more. Little kids get to go around being happy. The older a person gets, the more they have to focus on their future and doing what was right in their life. Life takes hard work in order to be successful, right?

So, Jalyn did not make any changes to her life. She buckled down and focused on her schoolwork, her team, and her family. But despite Jalyn's best efforts to return to normal, she could not shake the idea of her grandpa's to-do list. She never missed an "assignment" and that is what the list essentially was...an assignment. But it was the one list Jalyn had no idea how to create. That challenge, this struggle, bothered her. Why was this such a big deal? She could make her list in her mind no problem, but something about putting it down on paper was the challenge. Part of her knew that if she made that list, she would see a very different version of herself in it. She did what she had been doing every time she felt this uneasy feeling. She quieted her mind and started a conversation with God.

Speaking of things Jalyn couldn't shake, she tried her best not to have to spend time with Ethan. He texted her almost every day, and he would talk to her in the hallways. Jalyn felt drawn to him each and every time they talked. She secretly looked forward to, and hated, times with him. She wondered how that was even possible. How could a person both enjoy and hate time with someone? Why had she turned from this focused, successful person into someone who was being pulled in different ways in her life? She wasn't stupid - it all started after that conversation with her grandpa. She knew it had more to do with her than Ethan, and he looked crushed every time she made up an excuse not to go back and visit the pond with him.

She couldn't do it. She couldn't go back there. It was too much of a journey for her.

This charade went on for quite some time. Jalyn had found a way to avoid time at the pond and time with Ethan for almost a month. She just focused on her life and Jalyn was relieved when things went back to normal. She figured she was over that "self-searching" stage in her life and wanted nothing more than for things to stay comfortable.

Another thing Jalyn had avoided, or more forgotten about, was the English competition her teacher had told her about. She was so distracted with Ethan and lists that she had completely forgotten the competition. In English class the next day, Jalyn went to talk to Mrs. Ozark about the competition. Jalyn had long since made the changes to her paper, which much to her surprise, did actually strengthen her story. Mrs. Ozark had some great insights into the characters and plot direction. Her guidance had really made the characters stronger. Jalyn was quite proud of the final version of the narrative. But she had forgotten about the writing competition. Did she really feel comfortable enough to share her story? It was so personal. It was this thing created entirely in Jalyn's mind. What would people say? Her stomach rumbled as she wondered if she could handle criticism if people did not like the story? Plus, what good would it do to try for a writing competition. She knew her parents wouldn't care much about it. They put value in her sports, tutoring jobs, and math/science classes in the school. Writing to them was a hobby, a skill at best. They equated it to getting a job as an artist with part of a person's success being pure luck.

But Mrs. Ozark seemed determined to get Jalyn to try the

competition. "Jalyn, I wouldn't worry too much about the competition. If you don't win anything, that's okay. Writing is a very subjective thing. If anything, it will look great on your college applications, right?"

Jalyn could not argue with that logic and neither could her parents, so she agreed to enter the competition. She had to bring home a sheet of paper for her parents to sign, and there was a website where she had to submit her paper and fill out some forms. Looking at the form in her hand, Jalyn felt both excited and nervous at the same time. Here she was again trying something outside of her normal realm. She has got to stop making this a regular thing!

Later that night at dinner, Jalyn was waiting for the perfect time to tell her parents about the writing competition, but before she could, her dad asked her who Ethan was. Jalyn's heart stopped. "Why, Dad?" she asked.

"He stopped over today looking for you while you were busy after school," her dad explained.

"He's just a boy I know from school. That's all," Jalyn answered hoping to change the subject.

"What kind of student is he?" my mom asked. My mom was always interrogating us about the people we hung out with at school and outside of school. "You become who you hang out with, you know!" was my mom's regular saying.

Jalyn knew what she wanted to hear, but it wasn't the truth or maybe it was. Jalyn did not know anymore. She continued anyway. "He's a nice kid. Not very involved in school. More of a loner, but he is a decent student." Thanks to her, she thought to herself with a chuckle.

"Well, that's nice. Remember it is always good to be friends with everyone, but who you hang out with tends to influence the decisions you make, and you don't want to lose focus. You have some important college tests coming up, and you are doing so well in school. Don't get distracted. Boys are great," she winks at her husband, "But you have a lot of schooling ahead of you. Being a pediatrician takes a lot of dedication and work. Your grades right now are going to influence which college you go to and if you get scholarships or not. Just promise me you will focus, ok? You are such a good girl. Don't let anyone change that."

For some reason, these last two sentences left a pit in Jalyn's stomach. "Good Girl"…"don't change." This was the opposite of what grandpa was trying to get her to do. Her parents want her to stay the same, and Grandpa wants her to change. She loved being called a good girl before, but now it felt very…very… consuming. No one was good all the time. She was allowed to fail and disappoint people. She just wanted to be a girl. She just wanted to be herself. She felt like she was a rubber band being pulled in two different directions. But she shook it off and decided now was as good of time as any to tell her parents about the writing competition.

"I need to get your signature on a form for school," she started. "Mrs. Ozark gave it to me. You see, I wrote a story in her class, and she thought it was really good, and she wants me to submit it to the

Stenitzer National Writing Award competition. She thinks I can do really well." Jalyn felt a moment of happiness at this thought.

"Well, isn't that great," her dad added between bites of food, "Any award is a good award. It will look great on your college application."

"Of course it will. Great job, dear!" Mom said. "You should ask your other teachers if there are any award competitions you can enter for math or science. There has to be something for science at least. Writing a story is great, but if you are going to be a doctor, then you want to get some math and science accolades on your application as well," mom added and expectations came flying at Jalyn from across the table as her mom talked about the importance of getting into a good school, how it will impact her future, and ultimately her career. "Jalyn, I know it seems like a lot of work and pressure, but in the end, it will all be worth it. You have to work hard now, so in the future, you have the options you want for your life."

"What is the Stenitzer competition all about anyway?" Dad asked.

"I don't know a ton about it." She lied. She had actually read quite a bit about the competition. "I know that if you do well then there is this awards event you get to go to with some vendors and presentations. Seems pretty cool." She was lying again; it seemed *way* cool. It was almost like a writer's playground and it was not just for high school students. There were award winners from ages 5 up to adults. After the writer's expo there was a fancy awards ceremony and formal dinner. Part of Jalyn was longing to win and go to the event, but just as the excitement was building, her mom pulled her back to the real, practical world.

"That definitely sounds interesting, but realistically you don't want to be missing school, and I am not sure your dad or I could take off of work for that. We really need to save the days off of work and school for college visits. By the way, which one are we going to visit first this spring? I can't wait! Now that is something to get excited about, right, Jalyn?" Her mom started going on and on about the best program at University of *Whatever* and the percent of medical acceptance at *BlahBlah* College. Jalyn had only been half listening and half zoning out because she had heard this conversation a million times since she was little. It was drilled into her mind. She had been so thrilled when her brother finally decided on what college he was going to go to so the conversation shifted to another topic.

"Of course, Mom. Besides. I only think you go to the awards ceremony if you win, and I doubt that will happen," Jalyn confessed.

"Ok, well then, no problem. I'll sign whatever you need me to sign. I'll clean up dinner. Jalyn, why don't you head upstairs and get started on your homework."

Jalyn obeyed her mom and headed upstairs. But for some reason, she couldn't focus on homework. All she could do was look at the permission form Mrs. Ozark had given her. Her mind tossed around the idea of winning the award. This thought, this possibility, brought so much excitement to Jalyn's heart. The wanting and wishing for this award was too much for her to take in. Most of the things she wanted in her life were easy enough to attain through hard work. If she worked harder than everyone else, then most of the time she was successful. But this competition was different. No amount of hard work would guarantee her a win. Like Mrs. Ozark had said, writing is subjective, and the judges will either like her story or they won't. It was that simple. She did not like that her success was out of her hands. She had no control. She had to put her trust into someone else and just have faith.

Jalyn took out the blank to-do list she started for Grandpa, which she kept hidden under her mattress, and wrote under the side of things that made her happy. Jalyn added the word - writing. And she actually believed it. She let herself think about her experience of writing the story. It was bumpy and imperfect, but she loved everything about it- even the constructive feedback from Mrs. Ozark because it made the story better in the end. She didn't even care about the grade on the paper at this moment. It wasn't about grades; it was about doing something she loved. She was thrilled to submit her paper for the awards. Jalyn pushed her homework aside, grabbed her computer, and went online to submit the paper.

When Jalyn finally hit submit, she smiled. She felt content and calm. This was not a feeling Jalyn was used to. She realized too that her stomach was still full from dinner, which made her uneasy. She felt that rubber band pulling at her from both sides again. Ultimately, she felt compelled to find some level of control, so she went to the bathroom and sat in front of the toilet, but nothing happened. Something inside of her was holding the food in and she felt torn apart. Instead of expelling food, she started dripping tears. "No, no, no! This is not who I wanted to be. Stop it now!" Jalyn felt the voice from deep inside. She had never felt this way before. Something that had always given her strength suddenly seemed horrible. There were no rules in this situation and she felt lost. She sat on the floor of the bathroom with her back against the bathtub and prayed. "God, help me. Please help me. I have no idea who I am and what I am supposed to do. I need help!" She sat alone in silent sobs waiting for a response. When no answer came, she escaped without notice back to her room and shut the door. Her bed was her only source of comfort at this moment, so she grabbed one of her mom's sleeping pills and hid under the covers. Jalyn surrounded herself in silence and took deep breaths to calm her mind. As she tettered between consciousness and sleep, her thoughts wandered. She realized that she had a choice. The control she had was in making her own choices.

Jalyn popped up in bed and looked around. It was as if she was seeing the world for the very first time. She had a choice. Her choice was her control.

She did not have to be who she thought everyone else wanted her to be, but rather she could do what she wanted. This foreign realization brought tears to her eyes. The thought was so strange to her that she almost let the guilt slip back in for not purging her dinner, but she stopped it. Jalyn was doing things she had never done before. She wiped her face, laid back down and looked up. If she had always made decisions based on what others had expected of her, was she really in control of her life? Wasn't true control making decisions that she wanted for herself? Was she actually meeting any of her own expectations? Her mind was flooded and overflowing.

But she knew one thing...she reached under her bed for the to-do list again and wrote down something else under 'writing'; she wrote down 'full stomach'. Then she folded up the paper and put it back under her mattress.

And for the first time in months, she let herself think about the words Grandpa said to her. Jalyn closed her eyes and took a few deep breaths. It took a while to quiet her brain, but eventually, she talked.

"God," Jalyn said in her mind. "Thank you for everything you have blessed me with in this world. I know I am beyond lucky to have my family and school and friends. Please bless and take care of them." Jalyn paused. A lot of this felt very strange even if no one was listening. "I really don't know what to say. Grandpa said I should talk with you and ask for your help. I didn't really think I needed help, but Grandpa seems to think I do. I think I finally agree with him. Can you please help me figure out what makes me happy? Grandpa says that I should do something with my life that I am passionate about. But I have always known it was being a doctor. So I am not sure what he means, but he asked me to give this all to you and ask for your help. I know you are so busy and probably don't have time for this because it is not a big deal, but please help guide me to find my right path. Please help me see what my grandpa sees in me. Thank you, God."

She had no idea the spark of events she had set in motion. One day she would truly know that God was listening.

Ethan

"This is bullshit. Seriously," Ethan said to no one in particular after being blown off by Jalyn yet again.

It had been a while since he and Jalyn had talked by the pond. It was a life-changing kind of day, and Ethan knew Jalyn felt it too. But for some reason she has been working incredibly hard to blow him off ever since. Sure, she would stop and talk to him, but she made 101 excuses not to spend any amount of time together. He could feel the anger building inside of himself.

Just then, Ethan's mom walked in from work and asked him what was wrong. Ethan never talked to people about his feelings or thoughts. He was used to burying the feelings and ignoring his thoughts, but something had changed between him and his mom.

"I don't know, Mom," Ethan started not sure how much to say, "I hung out with this girl Jalyn at school, and we had a good time, but now she is doing everything in her power to ignore me. It makes me angry. What's wrong with her?"

Mom jumped in, "Ethan, don't give up on her. Give her some time, be patient with her. Everyone is fighting some sort of battle in their lives. It may not have anything to do with you. Most of the time you know nothing about it, but trust that she will come around in her own time," Ethan's mom explained, hoping some of what she said was getting through to the anger-filled Ethan. His mom knew that the changes in her son took some getting used to, and she imagined this girl at school felt the same way. She herself was waiting for Ethan to turn back into the angry, mean-spirited son she had, unfortunately, known for a long time. The kinder Ethan took some time to trust, but she knew he was worth it. Hopefully, this girl would feel the same way.

"What am I supposed to do in the meantime?" Ethan questioned.

"Well, instead of focusing on her, why don't you focus on you. You've been changing Ethan. I am not sure what sparked all of this, but, dear, these are amazing changes you are making. I am so proud of you. It's hard to change. It's hard to see the areas of ourselves that need work. Believe me, everyone has things they can work on, and most of us just ignore these sides of ourselves." She paused, "I know I do. What challenges are you facing? How can I help?"

"I don't know," Ethan added.

"Ok, let's try another approach. What makes you angry?" his mom asked.

Ethan sat and thought about this. It took a long time for him to respond, not because he struggled with the answers, but because he wasn't sure he was ready to talk about all this yet. Everything made him angry. It would be easier to tell her what didn't make him angry. Eventually, the answers started burning at his tongue and he had to get it out there.

"Fine. My dad, kids at school, and before, you...I mean, sorry...but it is true! Everything makes me angry!" Ethan blurred the words out like he had a bug in his mouth. But even with this information out in the open, Ethan did not feel any better; he actually felt worse.

"That's quite a list. Want to be more specific?" Mom pushed him, well aware that this pressure was probably going to upset him.

She was right. Ethan jumped off the bed, arms whipping about and started ranting, "My dad makes me so angry I want to punch a wall. He is always using me and everyone around him. He doesn't care about any other human on this planet but himself. I think he likes the idea of me, but not actually me as a person," he paused and continued talking, "I am mad at myself about you mom. You are always so damn nice to me, and I usually end up doing something mean to you. I don't mean to. I just can't seem to help myself. That's what happens with the kids at school too. No one really knows me. They know the version of me that I let them see from a far distance away. It's all freakin' bullshit. None of it is real. I pretend to be this tough guy. No one is close to me." Ethan dropped his eyes to the ground, "Except for Jalyn. I mean, we aren't close or anything, but she seemed to see me. She seemed to see the real me. She is the one that started me on this idea of getting to know the people around me, and it seemed to work," he looked at his mom, "It worked with you...but now she is blowing me off. Mom, I just want more, I want to be more. I feel worthless, empty, and I don't want to feel like this anymore."

At that, Ethan fell onto his bed, a ball of anger, sadness, and desperation. Mom knew that everything he said was true. Finally, he had acknowledged the truth in his heart.

She sat on the bed next to him. "Look inside yourself. Do you actually believe you are worthless?"

Ethan wanted so badly to say yes, but he knew it wasn't true. Or at least he really wanted to hope it wasn't true.

"Ok, then. Don't worry about Jalyn. She will come around. Trust me. You are worth fighting for. I know that is the truth through and through," his mom tried to calm Ethan. "In the meantime, let's work on the other areas. Let's start with the big one - your dad. What would have to happen for you not to be angry about him anymore?"

Ethan knew this was inconceivable, but answered anyway, "I guess he would have to start to care about me, or I would have to stop caring about him."

"Do you think either of those will happen?" Mom asked.

"Honestly, I don't know."

"Ok, so think about it this way. You were so angry until you started to get to know more about the people in your life. That insight helped you lower your anger. What if you took time to understand why your dad is the way he is? Maybe then you wouldn't be so mad at him."

While Ethan hated the idea of putting time and effort into his dad, his mom's idea wasn't so bad. "But, Mom, he was awful to you, and he is still awful to me. Don't you hate him? How could you not? He doesn't deserve anything!" Ethan could feel the blood racing to his face.

"You're right. He probably doesn't deserve any of that. But I realized a long time ago that forgiving him wasn't about him. It was about me. By forgiving him, and believe me, it took me a long time to swallow that idea...but by forgiving him, I found peace. I was able to let go, and that part of my life no longer had control over me. I could move forward without the past holding its grip on me, my mind, and my life. Maybe that can help you too. Why don't you call him now," urged Mom.

Ethan sat there for what seemed like an hour before he reached to grab the phone. He reluctantly picked it up and called his dad. Every ounce of him hated what he was doing, but what his mom said made sense. By the end of the conversation, Ethan had set up breakfast plans with him on Saturday. When he hung up the phone, his mom was smiling from ear to ear.

"Now let's figure out what you need to find out in order to understand more about your dad." Mom was not letting this go, and Ethan knew better than to try and end this conversation.

"I want to know why he sucks so bad. Can't I just ask you, Mom? You know him. Why go through him when I can just talk to you?" The questions were pretty straight forward.

"Because, Ethan, this isn't about me and you. Maybe we need to be more specific versus just wondering why your dad sucks. Your dad didn't start out this way, you know. Something in his life made him become the person you know today. It will take some time. Just think about it, Ethan." Mom knew she was not going to help Ethan unravel the mystery of his dad in one night.

Ethan took the next few days to think about what he wanted to ask his dad. Once Saturday morning came, Ethan was ready to get this over with. Every movement on the way to breakfast felt like a chore. There was not one part of Ethan that wanted to do this. His dad did not deserve this. It should be his dad making the effort, not Ethan.

Ethan arrived a little early, and once again, found himself secretly praying his dad would actually show up. He knew if his dad did not show, he would never get the nerve to try this again.

His dad did finally show up, and Ethan had no idea where to start. Ethan just sat there completely silent, but off course, his dad did not notice much. His dad just rambled on about him, him, him. After the waitress took their order, Ethan got up the nerve to begin. He had changed his questions a million times, but with his mom's help, he knew where to start.

So he started into his questions, hoping for some quick answer to his dad's suckage, but this was proving to be more difficult than he imagined. His dad dodged and slithered his way out of any direct answers. He was giving Ethan absolutely nothing to work with, and this was starting to piss him off to the point where Ethan slammed his hands down on the table sending the silverware sliding across the table.

"Seriously, Dad. What's wrong with you? You haven't been there for any part of my life. I think I deserve to at least understand why?" Now there were the questions Ethan really wanted to know about.

Ethan did not know if he was going to go into a rage, start to cry, or punch the wall, but he was filled with so many emotions that he finally exploded, and his dad sat there like a lump, not talking, not moving, just looking down at his food and eating. Eating! Ethan couldn't take it anymore.

"Screw you!! I am out of here. Don't plan on seeing me again. I am not going to sit here and listen to you talk about yourself nonstop. You scam and cheat on everything! Do you even know anything about me? Do you even care?" Ethan realized that people in the restaurant were starting to stare and look over at them concerned. "Mind your own damn business!" Ethan shouted to the restaurant as a whole.

Ethan got up to leave and was about to storm out of the restaurant when his dad started talking.

"Haven't been there for you? Talking about myself? What was I supposed to do? I've been struggling my whole life. It's all I know how to do. I scam and cheat, as you call it, to stay alive. It's just the way it is. It's just the way it is." His dad started very matter-of-factly, not really looking for any response from Ethan, not really even looking at Ethan.

Ethan was stunned at any level of realness coming from his father. "What do you mean? Why is it the way it is? It doesn't have to be. It didn't have to be. What the hell happened in your life that made you this way?" Ethan felt this questioning was a little harsh, but it is the only thing that made his dad actually start talking.

His dad went on to explain how he was in foster care for his entire life. He was passed from one family to another. He had to steal and survive however he could, use whatever means to get what he needed. A lot of the families he stayed with saw him as more of a burden than anything. When he was 18, he started living on his own. "I didn't know what to do. No one ever taught me how to get a job or what I was even qualified to do for work. Eventually, I met your mom, and she was the first great thing to come into my life. I wanted to be a good person for her, so I tried my damndest. And it was working. It was working until you came along. After you were born, she needed me to do more, be more, and I just didn't know how. I don't know if I wanted to know how. All she could do was nag me to get a job, nag me to help take care of you...I just couldn't do it. She made me so mad. I lost my temper more times than I could count. That's when I knew that I didn't know how to be a dad or husband," he paused slightly and swallowed hard before continuing, "I didn't want this life. It was too hard. I wasn't cut out to be a husband and a father. So, anyway," he continued snapping out of his past tale. "Anyway, now I do the best I can to get by for myself. I've got my own ways of doing things. You don't have to like it, but it works for me, and that is good enough for me."

Mom was right. The more his dad talked, the more Ethan's anger faded away. It wasn't because he liked what his dad had to say. In fact, it only made him realize that his dad never even tried to be a father. He gave up before he even started. He could have been a dad if he wanted to. So it was hard; life is hard. He tapped out and never even tried. Clearly, his mom wasn't worth it to his dad, and Ethan most definitely was not worth it to him. But somehow realizing that he needed to give up hope that his dad would become who he wanted. Somehow that made Ethan's anger start to disappear. Now he understood that there was no hope of changing his dad. How strange that this hope in his dad was causing so much anger, and once he understood who his dad really was... well, the idea of giving up hope that he would ever become a better person actually helped to calm Ethan. The anger he had felt for so long in his soul had left, oozing out of his heart and into the air. He accepted the situation for what it was and accepted his dad for who he was. That alone was enough to lessen his anger.

After leaving breakfast and coming home, he walked into the kitchen where his mom sat tapping her nails on the table. A habit she always did when she was nervous, and something she did every time Ethan met with his dad.

"How did it go, Ethan," asked his mom.

"Fine. But I don't think I am going to see him as much anymore. He made his choices in life, and now it is time for me to make my choices," Ethan said matter of factly.

"What did he say?" mom asked.

"A lot, and nothing at all. He talked about his rough childhood. About wanting to change when he met you. About realizing he was never going to be a good dad or husband. That he really didn't want to change." Ethan stopped and looked at his mom. "You were right. I do understand him more, and that made me less angry. It worked, but…"

"But…what?"

"Talking with him made me realize something. As he sat there telling me about himself," Ethan was embarrassed to even say the words, "I could hear myself in some of the things he said and see myself some of the things he did. I had never realized that before." A tear rolled down Ethan's cheek. "How did I not see this before? I am like him in so many ways, and I want to stop that. Right now."

"Ethan, the difference is you realize that you have a choice in who you are as a person. You get to choose the life you lead. You are being self-aware. That is a powerful tool. No one's perfect. We aren't meant to be. You always have a choice."

"I realize that now. Mom, I want to start being better. I know I can be better than Dad. I want to show people who I truly am. I want to be more."

"Here is the thing, Ethan, don't change for other people. You need to change for yourself, and that will have its own impact on other people. Make the changes you want within."

And with that, Ethan hugged his mom and headed upstairs.

Maddie

"Maddie, do you need help with number 7? Do you know what to do? Maddie, earth to Maddie?" Jalyn was not doing a great job this morning getting Maddie's attention.

"Maddie?!" Finally, Jalyn resorted to shaking her a little.

"Wha...What? Yes, I am ready."

"Ready for a nap maybe. You have no idea what I was even saying," Jalyn laughed. "What is going on with you, girl? You seem very, um, different lately. Don't you want to work on geometry now. Your parents pay me good money to make sure you know this stuff."

"Stuff is right. Let me ask you this, Jalyn, do you think college is really that important?" She knew this was a stupid question, even though teachers always said there were no stupid questions; this certainly seemed like one.

"Um, yea, it's like THE most important thing!" Jalyn looked at Maddie like she was crazy.

"Ugh! I am screwed then! Seriously, a superpower?! What good is a superpower if I hate school?!"

Fearing that Maddie was losing her mind, Jalyn moved the geometry homework aside, "What is going on? Talk to me? Maybe I can help you with more than geometry today. And why are you talking about a superpower?"

Maddie had not really thought of Jalyn as a real person. Well, obviously she was a real person, but not a person who cared about anything but school and her activities. She never thought of her as a friend. There was no way Jalyn could possibly understand Maddie's struggles. Jalyn was perfect, while Maddie was perfectly...screwed! But what the heck, she had nothing to lose.

"You see, my parents...and me, too...have wanted me to go to college on a softball scholarship. That's why they pay for tutoring and private coaches. All of that helps, but it is the only thing that works. Listen, me getting through school is kinda like a virtual reality game. When you are in the game the machine manipulates the situation so you can fly and do things you can't do in real life. Don't get me wrong, virtual reality is awesome, but it is still a game. Do you get what I mean?"

"No clue...sorry?"

"I get through school by you and my other tutors helping me. You guys hold my hand every step of the way. You are my virtual reality, and believe me school is definitely a virtual reality game for me. If I was left to do it on my own, the batteries would die, and my game would turn into reality. That's what is going to happen to me in college."

"But you can get tutors in college too. There is always someone there who can help."

"Tutors in high school. Tutors in college. Am I going to need tutors in my job too? I have a feeling the tutoring ends at some point in the real world. But that's just the thing, I don't want to do this anymore. I know I need to graduate high school, don't get me wrong, and I appreciate all your help, but there has to be something I can do that doesn't require a college education. Something I can do where I can be the 'Jalyn'," she shot Jalyn a look to make sure that was okay to say. Jalyn was smiling. "You get what I mean. I want to be the one with the right answer. I want to be the one who shines. I want to feel successful on my own without all the support getting me through."

"Of course there are plenty of things you are good at, Maddie! You are a stud on the softball field. Seriously, I have seen you play. You are spectacular!"

"Great, I can be a professional softball player. Then what? What would I possibly do after that? But the real truth is I do not want to go to college. With every ounce of me, I don't want to go to school. Softball or no softball, the thought of four more years of school, and we aren't even close to finishing high school, sounds awful. Like eating bugs awful."

Jalyn laughed, "Ok, ok, I get it. I don't really know what to say. What was the whole superpower thing about?"

"Well, my mom said everyone has a superpower. Something they do better than anyone else. She said sometimes school doesn't measure these superpowers, but they exist anyway."

This was a foreign topic to Jalyn. Being college-bound was all she knew, but she was determined to help Maddie. "OK, so what is your superpower, Maddie? Let's look up jobs that have that superpower."

Maddie blushed, she was really not sure about this whole sharing of vulnerabilities with Jalyn, but whatever. She was uber smart, so maybe she would know what to do.

"I have no idea. My friends say I am a good friend. That I really care and communicate well. I do feel like I can get a good sense of people, of who they really are on the inside. Maybe I can be a professional friend," she said as she let out a loud laugh.

Jalyn grabbed her laptop, "OK, let's search professional friend…" They both laughed. "No, seriously…jobs that require good people skills…communications…here we go…

- Clinical psychologists.

- Counseling psychologists.

- Customer service representatives.

- Doctors.

- Financial advisers.

- Human services assistants.

- Lawyers."

"College degree, college degree, college degree, college degree….There is no hope! I have no future!" Maddie knew this was true. "Ethan has no idea what he is talking about."

Jalyn seemed jump at the sound of Ethan's name. "Ethan? Ethan Waltz? What did he say?"

"I don't know. I ran into him down at the brook walk, and we were both kinda just talking about things, and I mentioned college, and he said a lot of the people in his life did not go to college, and they were doing just fine...better than fine, he said."

"Maddie, I'm sure there are plenty of jobs in this world that do not require a college education. Not everyone goes to school. I am sorry, but I am not sure I am the best person to ask about this. Why don't you talk to the guidance counselor, and…" Jalyn paused, "maybe talk to Ethan? He seems like he might have some good ideas for you."

"Okay, thanks, Jalyn. It was really nice talking with you this morning. Like, really nice." Maddie meant it too.

As luck would have it, Maddie nearly ran right into Ethan as she was walking out of the tutoring room with Jalyn.

"Ethan, how funny running into you. Literally, right? We were just talking…I mean…how are you?" Maddie recovered.

"Actually, I am doing pretty good. How about you?" Ethan looked genuinely happy to see her.

"Well…I was going to find you to see if I can get your help. You know when you mentioned that a lot of people in your family did not go to college? Well, can you tell me more about that?"

Just then the warning bell rang. "Sure, Maddie, of course. Now?"

"No, no time. How about I come over to your house after school today?"

Ethan hesitated, "How about I come over to your house instead? My mom usually doesn't like me to have people over." He looked down, and Maddie was not sure why.

"Of course. See you then." Maddie was a little more upbeat about things and really hoped Ethan could help unravel her future.

Before lunch, Maddie decided to stop in the guidance counselor's office to see what she had to say. Unfortunately, there were no appointments available, but she scheduled something for next week and took the pamphlet the secretary gave her. "Great, who knew my life's purpose and all my problems could be solved with a pamphlet!" Maddie stuffed it in her bag and laughed. At least she could laugh at her situation now. That was way better than carrying the weight on her chest. By the way, where was that weight? Ever since talking to her parents, the weight had been gone.

"Huh, that's weird!"

After school, Ethan showed up right on time. He looked incredibly nervous, which was funny to Maddie because she never really got nervous around other people.

"Hey, Ethan! How are you? Thanks so much for coming over. I just made some homemade potato skins. Want some?"

"Sure."

"Come on in. I love your car." The two of them started chatting as they walked into Maddie's kitchen. "Where did you get it from? You are so lucky to have a car. I borrow my mom's or dad's when they aren't using it. But, man, to have your own car...plus yours is a really cool car."

"My dad gave it to me, but I am thinking of getting rid of it."

"What?! You are crazy to do that."

"I know, right," Ethan looked at his car, "But let's just say I am ready to put the past behind me. Speaking of which, thanks for inviting me over today. Not sure I can be of much help, but I can certainly try."

Maddie watched in awe as Ethan devoured the potato skins. "These are amazing!" Ethan said in between shoveling in skins.

"Did you even taste them?" Maddie was amazed at the amount of food Ethan could eat in no time at all. "Now that is a skill!"

Ethan smiled a really genuine smile. Maddie had never really seen this look at Ethan before. Usually, he looked pissed off, and honestly, kinda scary.

"Okay. I need your advice, but how about we play a little catch while we talk? I need to loosen up my arm. I haven't pitched in a few days." Maddie was out the door, dragging Ethan by his arm before she even finished her statement.

"So what's up?" Ethan asked as he tossed the softball back to Maddie.

Maddie tossed the ball back. "You mentioned the other day that a lot of people in your family did not go to college. I am really, really, really looking for a future that does not include college, but most people I know are planning on going to college or junior college. I had always planned on this too. It just seems like the next logical step. It's what our teachers, parents, friends, and heck, society tells us to do. I know that some people will go to trade schools, but I don't really see myself as an electrician, welder, or mechanic. You know what I mean. Everyone else I have talked to about this doesn't know what other options there are out in this world. Did everyone go to college? If they did, they are better than me!"

"You really think everyone went to college? No way. My mom is a realtor, and she is pretty damn good at her job. She didn't go to college. There are a lot of jobs that still have schooling, but it is more like job training, so maybe that wouldn't bother you because it is not a traditional school. My aunt is a dental hygienist, which I think is a two-year program. My neighbor is a flight attendant, and he loves it because he gets to travel the world essentially for free. I know this guy that started working for a garden nursery, and now he does some job with a weird name with trees. He is even talking about starting his own business."

Ethan knew an awful lot of people who seemed successful without going to school, but none of those sounded like something Maddie could do or wanted to do.

"I don't know if those are jobs I could do" she said as she tossed the softball back to Ethan.

"Really? I don't know. You have a great personality, and you don't seem intimidated by people. My mom is always saying being a realtor is all about being able to develop good relationships. I don't know, that sounds like something you can do. If you want, I can talk to my mom to see if she can, like, show you her job?"

"Really? Sure!" Maddie couldn't help but smile at the thought that she had her first lead on a college-free future. She smiled as she caught the ball, "Ethan, don't take this the wrong way, but I have totally enjoyed this afternoon with you. I mean, we just never talked like this. You are a pretty awesome person, and not just because you are helping me, but this has been pretty cool. Thanks."

Maddie could see from across the yard that Ethan's face had turned a bright red.

"Maddie, you too...I mean, thanks. Me too."

"I am going to have to tell Jalyn about this in tutoring tomorrow. She will be so --"

Before Maddie could finish, Ethan jumped in, completely ignoring the ball and letting it hit the fence behind him. "Jalyn, why? I mean, what did she say? I mean. Sounds good. Never mind. Nothing." Ethan was talking as fast as he ate. Maddie knew what nothing and never mind meant. She just smiled.

"Oh, Jalyn is my tutor. We were talking about college-free jobs this morning. Honestly, I think it was a little out of her realm." Right then, Maddie remembered how Jalyn had responded when she mentioned Ethan's name. She pocketed that thought for later.

She and Ethan tossed the ball around for a while longer, talking about school, friends, music, and movies. Finally, Maddie's parents came home from work and yelled outside, "Hi, kids. Maddie, loosing up that arm? I like it! What's for dinner, Maddie? I'm starved."

"Well, the potato skins are out of the question," she said and laughed as Ethan buried his face into the mitt. "Just kidding, I started something completely different for dinner."

"You make dinner? I wouldn't have any idea what to do. If I made dinner, my mom and I would be eating cereal or frozen pizzas. Not really the dinner of champions," Ethan made a face at his own joke.

"I don't know. Cereal and frozen pizza totally work as solid dinners some nights!" Maddie explained, "My parents work long hours. I help out by making dinner. It works for us. Plus I like experimenting with cooking different meals. Sometimes it works, and sometimes it doesn't. Ha!"

"I should probably start heading home anyway. I'll talk to my mom tonight and text you. Thanks for today, Maddie, really. This was awesome!" Ethan said with a wave.

Maddie waved back, put the mitts away, and went inside.

"So, Maddie, who was that?" Mom said in a sing-songy way.

"Mooom, he is just a friend. Besides, I think there is someone else he likes." Maddie smiled to herself. "He was helping me figure out my superpower." She winked at her mom and started putting their dinner on the table.

Later that night, Maddie got a text from Ethan. "My mom said okay. She is excited to meet you."

Maddie smiled and pulled the pamphlet out of her pocket. "Why not?" and she started looking through it.

CHAPTER 7

Jalyn

By now, Jalyn had been making it a nightly ritual to talk with God before going to bed. At first, she was just doing it to follow what her grandpa had told her, but later she looked forward to talking out what she was experiencing every day. She was so thankful for the changes she had realized she needed. She felt like she was talking to a friend, but not exactly because she was the only one actually talking, but she felt God's presence and guidance in her life. It was an amazing feeling. She hated to admit it to herself, but she was realizing through these talks that she might not have all the answers. This was something she was going to struggle through, and for some odd reason, she was okay with that thought.

Part of what Jalyn realized was that she was blowing Ethan off. Well, that part was obvious to everyone. But she realized that she was ignoring him because he had seen her vulnerable. He had a window into the weak side of her and that freaked her out! Jalyn was never vulnerable -- not to her parents, or teammates, or friends. Everyone saw the strong version of herself. The version she let them see. "Nothing was wrong with that," she thought. "They all liked it better that way. They told her so. They loved that she was strong and capable, and most importantly, took care of her own stuff. People enjoyed that Jalyn required little work. She was positive and accomplished, and the world needed her this way. Being vulnerable and needy was not something the world was ready for or wanted at all. No one wanted to be around someone who required work, right? Showing weakness meant others had to help. No one has time for that." Jalyn ended her train of thought but this nagging feeling still sat with her. She knew she had to make things right with Ethan. She needed to talk to him. It wasn't his fault he caught her at a weak moment. He shouldn't feel bad because she hated to be seen as weak, so she cornered him in the hallway during school the next day.

"Hey, Ethan. I owe you an apology. Things have been weird. I have been weird. You shouldn't have to deal with my weirdness. I'm just trying to figure some things out. Anyway, how are you? I wanted to see if you wanted to hang out by the brook later today?"

Ethan just stared at her. This was unexpected. Ethan could barely keep up with the speedy delivery of her apology. Did she really just invite him to hang out? He knew this was too good to be true, but...he must be dreaming. This can't be real?! Still, she was standing there...real as anything. Eventually, he spit out, "Yeah??? okay. What time?"

"I'll text you. Thanks, Ethan. See you then!" Jalyn answered as she ran into the class just as the bell rang.

Later that day, Ethan and Jalyn met at the brook and exchanged awkward conversation. Neither one knew the right thing to say. They were both out of their comfort zones.

Finally, Ethan asked if Jalyn wanted to go sit by their pond.

Jalyn shyly smiled when Ethan said it was "their" pond. She agreed, and they started to walk. They walked together and arrived at the pond in silence. The quiet felt like an escape, and the two of them were so at peace with the quiet space between them. This place, this moment, just felt right. It had rained earlier that day, and Jalyn could feel the damp grass on her bare feet. Ethan had brought a plastic bag and blanket for them to sit on, which offered a safe, dry island in a field of dampness.

It was Jalyn who finally broke the silence. "Ethan, how are you?" It was a vague question, but the perfect question at that moment for Ethan to share what was on his mind.

"It's strange, Jalyn, I feel both better and worse right now. I enjoyed talking with you last time. I have to admit I was beyond happy to have had the chance to get to know you better. Then you, well…"

"I blew you off. I know it. You can say it," Jalyn broke in.

"Yes. It was really hard to deal with because I have to tell you that the idea you gave me…about learning new things about the people in my life, well, it helped. It helped a lot. My mom helped too."

Ethan could tell that Jalyn was happy to hear this, so he went on. "In fact, it was my mom's idea that I should give you space and not get angry that you were blowing me off. She made me realize that I might take some...getting used to. I know I treated you horribly before, Jalyn. I can say sorry forever. But I have changed. You don't have to believe me, but I have, and you helped start the change in me."

Ethan could tell that Jalyn had gotten more than she expected from the "How are you?" question.

"I've been working on me." Ethan had no idea why it was so easy to open up to Jalyn. "I realized a lot of my anger had to do with my dad. I used your two-questions method with my dad too. I met with him and found out some stuff about who he was. Somehow knowing him better, understanding him, has made me hate him less. I don't like him, but I don't have so much anger. Shocker, right?"

Ethan laughed nervously, even though nothing he said was funny. He just wanted Jalyn to know he had changed and changed for the better.

"That's a good thing! Wow, that had to have been a tough conversation!" Jalyn chimed in picking at the clovers in the grass.

"It was, and it wasn't...It was just something I needed to do. But anyway, it made me realize I am ready to be different, ready to figure out who I am." As soon as Ethan said these words, Jalyn saw his face flush. Jalyn knew the feeling and noticed the pile of clovers she had picked by her side.

"So who are you?" Jalyn tried to keep him going. She had been so embarrassed that she was vulnerable around him, but that thought was long gone from her memory.

"I am not even sure where to begin. I want to just be more myself with the kids in school. I want to do more. I just want to be like everyone else. I have spent so much time pushing people away that I have no idea how to even get people to want to know me better?" he paused then added, "How do you do it, Jalyn?"

This surprised Jalyn. "Me, how do I do what?"

"You're a normal student and do normal stuff. Well you are probably an above-average student doing above-average stuff, but still...I want to be more like you. Sorry, is that weird?" He tossed a rock aside as he tried to avoid her eyes.

"No, not at all." He was certain Jalyn had no idea how to reply to his completely honest and completely insane request. She continued, "I can help you with that!" Jalyn wasn't sure where to go next with this conversation, and the quiet returned.

"You know, Ethan. I think I know how you feel. Not about being involved in school, but wanting to just be happy to me more...real. Just be content and not worry so much. I get that. But you know how we are different?" Ethan could list at least 10 ways he and Jalyn were different, but there was no way he was going to say that! So he nodded, and Jalyn continued, "You want to connect more with the kids in school, and I want to stop worrying about what other people and kids in school think of me. I have no idea how to be the type of person who doesn't carry every sense of myself in what others think of me." She blushed.

"Are you afraid to change?" Ethan asked. "I know I am."

Jalyn did not want to say the words aloud, but she finally did, "If I change and put the things I want first, then people will just forget about me. I will be meaningless. People, all people, like me because I work hard to make them happy. I work harder than everyone at everything I do. If I stop that, then everyone will stop caring about me. I will just be...ordinary. What if who I want to be doesn't measure up to what others expect from me? What if ordinary makes me forgettable to everyone I know?" Jalyn blushed again, but Ethan could tell this was her truth.

Ethan jumped in right away. "Really? You don't think you measure up? Seriously? You need to not be so worried about other people. Look at me. I've been an ass for so long, and there are still people who haven't given up on me. I think you are underestimating the people in your life and yourself. To be honest, most people in school like you in spite of your constant 'know-it-all-ness!'" Ethan laughed, but quickly looked at Jalyn hoping he did not upset her by this comment. "No offense."

Actually that comment made Jalyn laugh at herself. Maybe what Ethan said was true. She would have to really think about all this. "I never really thought about it that way. I guess I have always been kind of a 'know-it-all,' but I like knowing it all. I am always surprised at how much everyone else *doesn't* know." They laughed.

"Okay, back to you, Ethan. You realize that people at school have never given up on you, right? People are drawn to you, even if you are an ass sometimes." She smiled a little knowing that is how she had always felt about him. "No offense," she said with a wink.

"They respond to you. You don't seem to care what others think, and that intrigues people. Most of us don't think that way. Heck, how many teenagers do you know that don't care what other people think? You have a strong personality. You need a strong personality to be a good leader." Suddenly she had a great idea and screamed, making Ethan jump back and the birds fly out of the tree near them.

They both laughed.

"I can help you! I can totally help you! You said you wanted to be more like me, why don't you work with me on some of the school officer projects. I can introduce you to some people, and you can get more involved in school. I can always use some help! Maybe that is too dorky for you but it definitely gets you out doing more. What do you say?"

Jalyn knew it was a perfect plan, and it seemed like Ethan was actually open to the idea.

"Maybe we can help each other. In a weird way, you can help me be more like you, and I can help you be more like me."

Jalyn looked at Ethan for his reaction, then she looked down. She knew this seemed true. It was a very honest statement. Ethan nodded and simply said, "Yes. I'd like that."

They stayed there for another half hour talking and sharing. As the sun started ducking behind the trees, casting a shadow on their blanketed spot, they knew it was time to head home. As they walked back to their cars, they talked. Soon Jalyn slowly and nervously found a way to grab Ethan's hand in hers.

"Jalyn, this… Thank you. You are someone special. I am glad I stopped bugging you for homework. These conversations are much better than answers to some stupid homework assignment." Ethan wondered where these words came from, but he knew they were true.

"Me too, Ethan. I like this better than handing over my hard-earned answers." He laughed and winked at her. Not the kind of wink his dad used to give when he was hiding some slimy truth, but a wink that said she meant something to him. A wink that meant that they shared something special together. That's a wink he would never forget.

"Goodbye, Ethan." Jalyn waved goodbye and in the back of her mind, she had hoped he would kiss her. Ethan felt the same way but remembered the last time he tried to kiss a girl.

He waved back at her, and with that, Jalyn drove home fully aware she had been gone longer than she intended.

Once she got home, her mom met her at the garage door. "Jalyn, where have you been? I texted you at least five times!"

In the hazy of her time with Ethan, Jalyn had completely forgotten to check her phone. "I was at the brook hanging out with Ethan. Sorry, Mom. I am actually going to help him get more involved in school. It's a good thing."

"That's all fine, dear," she seemed content with Jalyn's answer. She quickly switched subjects to the real reason she was texting her daughter. "But I am worried about you. I noticed you got a B+ on your math quiz. Some of your other grades have dropped a bit too," her mom said plainly, but Jalyn knew there was a question there.

The truth is Jalyn had noticed her grades too, but she still had an A average, so she didn't let it bother her. Along with studying every night, she had been spending each night working on her to-do list and talking Preston on her volleyball team. The two of them had bonded at a sleepover and confided in each other that they both had an eating disorder. Jalyn didn't quite call it that, but Preston did. The two had been giving each other support and helping each other make healthier decisions. While she was losing some homework time, it wasn't enough to drastically affect her grades. So she wasn't this amazing superstar A+ student each day in class; she was kind of liking this more relaxed mode of school.

"Jalyn, I didn't want to mention this either, but I noticed...well...maybe you should start exercising a little more. You know now that volleyball season is over," her mom stopped abruptly, "Exercise is always good for you. Good for all of us."

This too was something Jalyn was noticing. In her effort to stick to her to-do list of happiness, she wanted to keep enjoying a full stomach, which meant she had put on a little weight. Meal time had become a constant Dr. Jekyll and Mr. Hyde moment for her. She never knew which side would win over, and this had been a huge challenge for her. It was taking some time and lots of conversations with Preston, but Jalyn had finally come to accept that her purging "tool," as she once thought of it, was actually an eating disorder, and she did not want that in her life anymore. She had always thought she was happy, but was throwing up every night really a sign of happiness? It seemed so obvious to her now. It wasn't back then. It was a little tough to deal with because while she felt better eating and keeping food in her stomach, she was losing the perfect size 2 she always thought she had to be. But again, she was kind of okay with this, but she did want to be healthy physically too.

Jalyn had no interest in telling her mom all of this. Vulnerability was not her family's strong suit. So she just said, "You're right, Mom. Maybe I'll talk to the volleyball girls and see if they want to set up a workout group after school." Jalyn was ready to end this conversation, so she told her mom she had homework to do and headed upstairs.

As Jalyn went into her room, she shut the door and pulled out grandpa's list from under her bed. It wasn't really a to-do list any more. It was becoming her to-be list. The list of things she wanted in her life. She grabbed a pen and added two more things to the list.

<u>Things that make me happy</u>

- Writing
- Full stomach
- Being healthy
- Helping others.

She truly meant that last one. In all her time tutoring other people, she really did enjoy seeing others succeed. She was looking forward to helping Ethan get more involved. He really did have everything he needed to be a great leader. She just knew it. It's just that no one had heard this part of his story yet, and maybe now they could work together to help tell the next part of his story.

Ethan

Ethan sat at his kitchen table reliving the past few months. All of it was so strange, and he felt like he was living someone else's life. The Ethan he always knew, the Ethan everyone knew, was not who he felt like today. He felt so relieved today when Jalyn had asked him to meet her at the brook. She made him feel so calm, and with her there, he felt like he could be the person he wanted to be. He tossed around the idea she had said about him helping her on some projects at school. Being involved had never been Ethan's thing, but it did seem to make sense that it was one way to get to know more people. He had always admired Jalyn's drive to be the best and give the most to everything she did. Maybe he could learn to be more like that. Quite honestly, he was so surprised to hear Jalyn tell him that she doesn't want to be that person. That she felt like she had to be a certain way to make others happy. She had always seemed so in control, so in charge of her life. "Huh, I guess Mom was right. Everyone is fighting some sort of battle, and most of the time, we know nothing about it."

His thoughts were interrupted by his mom coming in the door from work. He looked forward to these times with his mom. While he would never probably admit it to her, he had been working hard lately to be more kind to her.

"What a crazy day! How was your day, Ethan?" His mom poured a glass of wine and sat down at the kitchen table beside Ethan ready to talk.

Ethan wasn't sure how much of his day he should share with his mom. He had only really mentioned Jalyn that one time. Since Jalyn had blown him off for so long, there wasn't much to talk about...until now. So he decided he would tell his mom about meeting up with Jalyn at the brook. He told her all about who Jalyn was and that they thought they could help each other be more like the other person. He went on and on, giving his mom almost every detail about the day.

Ethan's mom's face was full of shock at Ethan's honest conversation, but she quickly recovered herself and said, "She sounds like a wonderful girl. I would love to meet her sometime. Maybe she can come over for dinner later this week?"

"Sure, I'll ask her. But, Mom, she wants to help me meet more people and get more involved in school. Do you think I *should* do that?" Then he asked the question he really was wondering about. "Do you think I *can* do that? It sounds stupid, but will people really accept me if I suddenly start acting different? I have perfected the ability to push people away and keep them at a distance. This is all just so new to me."

"Don't underestimate the people around you. Plus, Ethan, you probably won't believe this, but I was quite involved in school back in my day. I loved being in clubs and hanging out with different groups of friends. You know, I could help you too."

This was all news to Ethan, and he couldn't help but ask, "Thanks, that would be great, but Mom, no offense, but you never hang out with friends. I know you meet with lots of people for your job, but I had no idea you liked being social?" He immediately felt sorry for being so blunt, but it was true.

His mom took some time before she responded. She almost seemed to be having the conversation in her head before saying it aloud.

"Ethan, you're right. I guess we both need a little help in this area. My work comes easy to me, but trusting people enough to build friendships, well, I guess it has been a while."

Ethan leaned over and hugged his mom. He couldn't help feeling a twinge of guilt that maybe his mom didn't have many friends because of him.

"So what are we going to do with ourselves?" his mom laughed. "By the way, I reached out to your friend Maddie. She is going to come over this weekend to talk. I like her. She has a great personality! Ethan, you definitely attract some great friends!" She rubbed his hair like she used to when he was a little boy. "But before we figure out how to meet more people, first, we eat!" She leaned backwards and grabbed a pizza from the counter. "Only the finest cuisine for us tonight. The best pizza Westwood has to offer. I will only accept the finest for my son." They laughed and ate a slice.

But Ethan knew this was true. His mom had always had his best interest at heart. Everything she did was for him. Ethan vowed to work to be more selfless like his mom and erase the ways he was like his dad. That thought felt really good inside.

Maddie

Maddie had sat down with her mom to talk about meeting Ethan's mom and looked over the pamphlet she got from school.

"Mom, Ethan talked about a lot of jobs where you go to school, but not really school. You basically do job training, which is different from school. I think I can do that."

Her mom was studying the pamphlet. "Maddie, whatever you do, if you give it your all, you will be amazing. We have always supported you and given you everything you need to be successful at what you told us you wanted. You know that, right? We never wanted you to feel pushed into anything."

Maddie hugged her mom. "Mom, I know, you and dad are always my biggest cheerleaders. But, honestly, in today's world, how did I ever think that not going to college was an option?"

Her mom knew this was true. "I know. And your dad is struggling with this still. There is a certain level of comfort with having a bachelor's degree, but it doesn't necessarily guarantee success either." The two of them sat there together, deep in their own thoughts.

"Hey, Maddie, have you really looked at this pamphlet? There are some interesting jobs in here that have job training without the four-year schooling. Chiropractor, hair stylist, makeup artist, medical assistant, elevator repair, sales account manager...that sounds interesting. I would buy something you were selling!" Maddie leaned into her mom and started reading the pamphlet over her shoulder.

"I am not sure, Mom. Let me meet with Ethan's mom and see what she has to say. Maybe selling houses could be my future." Maddie stood up in a regale stance and a winning smile, "Come sell your home with Maddie Lopez, Westwood's premier real estate agent!"

Maddie fell onto her bed, and she and her mom sat looking through the pamphlet envisioning the many opportunities for Maddie's future.

Her mom had given her the hope, courage, and questions she needed to knock on Ms. Waltz's door that Saturday morning. She knew this visit was important and possibly critical to her future. She appreciated that Ethan's mom was willing to sit with her, so she had baked her some of her delicious caramel fudge brownies as a thank you.

After three knocks, Ethan opened the door all smiles and welcomed Maddie into his home. It was a cute place, and Maddie could see Ms. Waltz sitting in her office around the corner.

"Ethan, thanks so much for your help. I made these for you and your mom."

"Come on in. Mom's waiting for you. Mom, this is Maddie." Ethan pointed to Maddie, and she knew that was her cue.

"Ms. Waltz, thanks for taking time out of your busy schedule to help me. Here," she presented the brownies. "I made these for you as a thank you. You have no idea how much this means to me.

"Please, Maddie, call me Lynda. These look delicious, my dear. You did not need to do that, but I am sure we will love them! Come in, come in. Sit down. I have so much to show you. But first, tell me about yourself."

So Maddie went into her song and dance about school and softball, her dad's hesitations about all of this, future plans, blah, blah, blah. At the end of it all, Ms. Waltz had a big smile on her face. "Maddie, I can't tell you how happy I am that you talked to Ethan and had the courage to ask questions. There is so much pressure for kids to go to college these days, but there are millions of jobs out there. I get what your dad is saying, but do you know how many people with a bachelor's or even master's degree work in my office? Unfortunately, when so many people have degrees, sometimes it waters down the value. I am not knocking college education, absolutely not, but we need all kinds of jobs to make the world go round. We need people to collect our garbage, organize our grocery stores, cut our hair, run local businesses, and fix our air conditioners when they go out. These are critical jobs, and none of them require a college degree. Now don't get me wrong, you will need job training and most of these jobs have rigorous certification processes you need to complete in order to be successful. These jobs are not easy, and they all require a special person with special skills. But, in the end, you do not have to have the traditional four-year education that colleges provide. So what do you think?"

"I do not mind working hard. I just want to find a career where I can stand on my own two feet and be successful. Right now, I make it through school because of my tutors, and while I so appreciate them, I don't want that for my future. I want to be a success because of me and my own work. I have to believe I have some skills that the world needs?"

"Of course you do, Maddie. How about we enjoy some of your brownies and have some tea while I tell you a little bit about my job." With that, she poured some tea and placed a brownie on each of two plates. Maddie sat, ate, drank, and listened to Ms. Waltz as she told Maddie all about the world of real estate. Maddie had to admit it sounded like an exciting job with lots of people interaction, paperwork, negotiation, and market-watching. Maddie really felt this was something she could do. Ms. Waltz had even offered to take her out on a few client meetings. Everything was shaping up well when she finished telling Maddie about real estate, sat back, and sipped her tea and ate her brownie.

"Maddie, oh my gosh, wow...these brownies are ridiculously good. Like the best brownies I have ever tasted - good!" Ethan heard his mom from the other room and yelled, "You should try her potato skins. I've never tasted anything as good. Sorry, mom, no offense."

"No offense taken. If her potato skins are half as good as her brownies, then there is no way any of my meals could even compete."

Maddie smiled. She loved it when people loved her food.

"Do you cook and bake often, dear?"

"I love trying out new recipes and ingredients. It started out as a kind of a chore to help my parents out when they worked late. I guess I got pretty good at it, and now I just enjoy making food for people. I love seeing the looks on their faces as they take a bite into what I've made. I enjoy being with people, and I guess making food is another way to enhance my friendships and relationships with others."

Ethan stood in the doorway, and his mom sat in her chair. They both had these weird grins on their faces. They looked at each other and looked back at Maddie. It was very bizarre. Almost like they had a secret between them that that hadn't shared with her.

"I almost forgot about your famous Maddiecakes. Mom, people talk about them all the time at school. She makes them for breakfast, and they are to die for." Ethan was beyond excited, like he had discovered a new land. Maddie was still utterly confused about what all the excitement was about.

"Maddie," Ms. Waltz looked straight at her. "Everyone wants a job they love, right?" Maddie nodded. "You told me you wanted a job you could stand on your own two feet without needing a tutor or help to be successful, right?" Maddie nodded again. "Maddie, you realize that there are many, many successful chefs in this world. People pay lots of money to eat foods made by great chefs, and the Westwood Area Junior College has an amazing culinary arts program."

There were no words. Maddie could barely form any thoughts. She could hear every breath she took. These words sat in her head, just waiting to be fully absorbed into her brain.

"A chef?"

Maddie's mom had said everyone had a superpower, something a person does better than anyone else. Never, never had Maddie even thought that cooking was her superpower, but people did seem to think she did it better than most. This almost seemed too good to be true. She did not know what to say.

"But I came here to learn about being a realtor?" She felt like she was being rude to Ms. Waltz.

"Are you kidding me? You came here to discuss your future, and I think, together, we nailed it! Nothing is better than that! You are welcome to still learn about real estate, but I think we both know what you would enjoy more."

Ethan and his mom looked pretty pleased. Maddie sat there in a state of disbelief and bliss. Working as a chef would be amazing. Could that really be a job? Cooking never felt like a job to Maddie. She could envision herself in a big kitchen, quickly maneuvering between pots and plates. She loved everything about the idea of creating delicious meals every day of her life. The calmness of being in the kitchen, the endless online resources and recipes, the adventure of switching up ingredients, and trying new things. If she could spend her life doing this...that would be the best career ever!

"I have no idea how to thank you. I do, I think this might be just about perfect. It is not something I have ever thought about before, but I definitely will now!"

Maddie sat up and gave Ms. Waltz and Ethan a hug. "This has been one of the best days ever. Thank you so much!"

"No problem, just promise me one thing, Maddie," Maddie nodded, "Promise to give me reservations on the opening day of your famous new restaurant."

Maddie was beaming from ear to ear as she walked out of Ethan's house. She could not wait to go home and talk with her parents. She could not wait to tell them that she discovered her superpower, even more than that, she had a passion for the future.

CHAPTER 8

Jalyn

"Did you get the tickets for lunch today?" Jalyn asked Ethan as they met to talk at her locker.

"Yep. I hope you don't mind, but I made a form for people to fill out so we can track who purchased which items for the fundraiser. It will make things so much easier when we go to organize all the information by homerooms, and then it will be so easy to hand out the items."

"Mind? Mind? Are you kidding? That is brilliant! Ethan, you are a genius. And what is that on your face? Looks like a big smile. Be careful, mister tough guy, I think people may start to think you like this stuff," Jalyn teased. "Ummm...you're welcome!" she laughed and winked at Ethan.

Ethan had grown to love hearing Jalyn laugh. He didn't remember hearing it in the past; maybe he just wasn't paying attention?

"You may have given me this chance, but it is my super-genius ideas that are getting you more organized and cleaning up your messes! So *you* are welcome!" Ethan messed up Jalyn's hair as he ran off to get to class.

Jalyn couldn't help but smile to herself. He was still a pain in her ass, but he could make her laugh like no one else. He loved to tease her in such a way that made her able to laugh at herself. She was able to not take herself too seriously when she was with him. That was a new feeling, and she loved every minute of it! This was beyond refreshing, and so new to her. She really enjoyed being a little more chill and not so worried all the time. She was slowly changing, and while it felt so good. She couldn't help but feel like she was becoming a little more of a slacker. She couldn't really talk about this to anyone but, let's be real, her slacking was probably someone else's best day. But for her, life was a little different these days.

Teachers seemed a little disappointed when she wasn't the first one raising her hand with a perfectly poised answer, but she still got great grades. Her friendship with Preston was strong, vulnerable, and honest. She had been spending more time with her volleyball friends, and they were loving working out together. Jalyn wasn't sure why, but they seemed so much more relaxed around her, which made Jalyn look so forward to their time together. Her healthier lifestyle had caused her to have to buy some new clothes, but she could still see the concern in her mom's eyes. But her dad noticed that she had a special glow to her these days.

Jalyn just sat in the middle of the cafeteria, looked up, and smiled. A giant, heart-wide-open smile. "God, thank you. I know this feeling is because of you. I used to think you were not listening, and you had no reason to help me, but you did. I know it was your guidance in my life. You have brought this light into my body and happiness into my heart. You are great and never need to prove anything, but you did. You showed me, told me, that you were here, and I am worth your love. You have helped me on my way and opened the doors for me. Oh, God, thank you. Thank you for letting me feel this and see this." Jalyn realized she was smiling, crying, and praying right there in the middle of the cafeteria, but she didn't care. This was too amazing, too powerful of a moment not to experience it right here, right now. Jalyn was experiencing the power of God in her life, and she was beyond overwhelmed and enveloped in awe.

Her grandfather had told her all about this, but she did not understand what he meant until she experienced it herself. It took time, trust, and patience to let God do his will in her life. She had always thought of God as an authority, someone who watched over her and determined whether she was living her life according to His rules. She felt that religion was there to judge people and keep them in line. But what she was experiencing was so much more. It went beyond religion and rules; it was a relationship with an all-loving God. He does not judge; He just loves. Grandpa once told Jalyn that God made each of us. He knows all our good things and bad things. He accepts us just as we are and wants us to be the true version of ourselves. We do not need to pretend or be anything other than who we are. Grandpa had started her on this journey after seeing the struggles in her. She was so thankful for his conversation by his car that one night.

With her grandpa's help, Jalyn had even started writing more stories.

It took a while, but Jalyn finally got up the nerve to talk to her grandpa about her to-be list and her prayers. She was quite nervous to talk about them out loud, but it became easier and easier. She felt bad because she knew she was hiding a part of herself from her parents, but she saw no other way. They just did not get her and the changes she was experiencing.

At one of her hardest moments, her grandpa had told her that every tough time in his life brought about a greatest part of his life. It was hard to believe, but what he said was true. She hoped this would be the same with her life. This was certainly the hardest thing she had gone through. She was changing a lot of her life, and her parents were not exactly supportive. Grandpa encouraged Jalyn to talk to her parents, and she did, but it never turned out that well. He said give them time because they loved Jalyn, and they wanted what is best for her, but they just wanted her to follow their path. They knew that their path had brought about much success. "Give them time to understand your path. They will come around. I promise," Grandpa had said.

While most of Jalyn's classes were changing, English was no exception. Mrs. Ozark had become a great mentor, and Jalyn would visit her during lunch to discuss books or exchange thoughts on Jalyn's latest stories. While sitting in English class one day, Jalyn couldn't help but laugh a little when she remembered how she had freaked out that day Mrs. Ozark had red-lined her paper with changes. She was so afraid of being wrong, but now she realized it was more about learning new things and building ideas into even stronger ideas. "Hmm. It's crazy how things have changed." Jalyn almost did not recognize the girl she used to be. She loved that girl and knew how hard she worked, but while Jalyn still worked hard, she did not feel spent and pulled in different directions. Jalyn chose her direction and her focus. She spent time doing things that made her happy. As Jalyn continued to daydream, Mrs. Ozark came over and asked if she could talk with Jalyn after class that day.

"Jalyn, have a seat. I don't even know where to start...I am not even sure how to say this..." Jalyn had gotten used to Mrs. Ozark's unique level of expression. She often got so excited that she could barely get the words out.

"What? What's going on?"

"Jalyn, your paper, your story..." she calmed herself, and continued with a smile, "Your story won third place in the writing competition in the young adult short story category. I am exploding with excitement for you. You should be so proud of yourself. This is an amazing honor. You have been invited to the awards reception in California. No one from our area has ever won this award before!" At that, Mrs. Ozark screamed and hugged Jalyn.

Jalyn's mind was racing, she had honestly forgotten about the competition. There was no way she had ever expected to hear back from them, let alone win third place. "Really? How did you find out? When did you find out?"

Mrs. Ozark explained, "I received a letter in the mail today. You will probably get one at home. Oh, I hope you don't mind that I told you. Maybe I should have waited for you to go home and get your letter. I am just so excited for you. I wanted you to find out as soon as possible. But go home, check your mail. Talk to your parents about making arrangements, then just let the awards committee know how many tickets you want for the event," she screamed, "Ah, I am just so happy for you. This is something special, Jalyn. This is something special."

Jalyn was filled with so much pride and happiness. She had experienced a lot of success in her life, but something about this felt more genuine. She had put her story out into the world. A story that she created and wrote with no idea how people would respond. Her writing was something she did for herself, and now it seemed to be taking on a life of its own. It was awesome and overwhelming. This was an amazing feeling of happiness, but even the word happiness did not seem to do it justice. She made a mental note that she needed to come up with a new word to describe this strong feeling of genuine realness and happy contentment.

As soon as she got home, she raced to the mailbox, tossed her backpack down right in the middle of the street, and ripped open the letter from the competition. She read it as quickly as possible, and she could see that she had won third place in the young adult short story category and that she and her family were invited to a reception on April 1st in California.

"April 1st!! April 1st!!"...her heart sank. April 1st was the date of the senior class officer debates. If she missed the debates, she could not run for class president, and that had been her goal since freshman year. Her family was so excited that she may give the big speech at graduation. It was something they were all looking forward to.

As she walked into the house her mom asked her what was in the mail. "Nothing exciting," Jalyn lied. She took the letter, went straight to her room, and shoved it under her mattress, right next to her to-be list. She would have to deal with that later.

Ethan

The three of them sat at the table laughing and enjoying the dinner that Mrs. Waltz had made that night. This has become a regular thing...Ethan, Jalyn, and his mom having dinner together. Ethan's mom had come to like Jalyn almost as much as Ethan did. There was a warmth and vibrancy to the house that had not been there before.

Ethan and Jalyn had been spending more time together, and Ethan could feel her getting stronger by the second. He knew she was definitely helping him too because he hadn't been angry for a long time. It was a slow process for him and everyone around him. Not everyone at school took to the new version of Ethan right away. People don't tend to trust someone when they suddenly start acting differently. But regardless of their reaction, Ethan just kept moving forward and giving them time to get to know the real him. He worked hard to be honest and straightforward with everyone he talked to at school. He stopped asking anyone for homework answers and hadn't gambled in a long time. Ethan made sure to sit with new people at lunch and worked hard to start conversations with others. When in doubt, he always went back to what Jalyn told him about learning two new things about the people in his life. He would ask people about themselves, and he realized pretty quickly that people loved to talk about their lives. This worked out well for him because Ethan was new to this whole socialization thing. He learned an awful lot about his classmates. The things he wanted to know, and things he didn't want to know.

His friendship with Jalyn was different than anyone else. He never worried or wondered what to say. It all came so naturally with her, and they never seemed to care about the silence. In fact, the quiet times were when he felt most connected to her.

Jalyn was involving him in a lot of projects at school too. Who knew how much that girl accomplished in one day. He was volunteering at fundraisers, making ghosts out of suckers for Halloween sales, and dressing like an elf for holiday grams. At times he just had to laugh at this strange version of himself he had become, but although it was different, he kind of loved it. He loved waking up in the morning with a purpose and importance in the world. He enjoyed having people smile when they saw him, which was the complete opposite of when they used to look away from him quickly to avoid eye contact in the past. His world was so different these days.

But tonight was going to be another first. It was one thing to make small talk in the hallway, but tonight, with the encouragement of Jalyn and his mom, Ethan was having a group of people over for a bonfire. While this may be normal for most high schoolers, this was one of the first times Ethan had invited a group of friends over since 5th grade. To say he was nervous was the understatement of the year! It's true he would go to the occasional party or social gathering, but there was so much going on he could pop in and out of conversations as he wanted and leave whenever he grew bored of his classmates. He felt better knowing Jalyn would be there with him, and his mom had pulled out all the stops and even went a little overboard! His counter was covered with enough snacks and food to feed the entire town, let alone a small group of friends. She even set up a s'mores bar with marshmallows, graham crackers, and a variety of candy bars and ingredients to use in the s'mores. There were so many creative combinations on that counter. Maddie had told Ethan's mom about this idea, and she loved it!

The next thing Ethan heard was the doorbell ringing. He looked at Jalyn and noticed how pretty she looked tonight. She was always pretty, but now she was special to him and that made it hard to look away from her. She squeezed his hand. "You got this!"

With that, Ethan headed to the door with a true smile on his face. "Hey, come on in. Thanks for coming!"

The first person to arrive was Maddie. She waved hi to Ethan and Jalyn and ran over to Ethan's mom. They were deep in conversation and pointing from one s'mores ingredient to another when the next guest arrived. One by one people arrived, and the party moved outside.

The weather that night was perfect with a bright moon and silent wind. As the fire danced around the stones, Ethan moved just as smoothly around the party, engaging each guest in conversation, and solidifying himself in the middle of many growing friendships.

Maddie, in her Maddie way, was walking around sharing the creative s'more ideas they had crafted, and people were eating it up - literally!

Everyone was having a great time, including Ethan.

"Hey, you!" Ethan snuck up behind Jalyn and squeezed her shoulders. Little did he know this sent a shiver up her body.

"Hey, yourself!" Jalyn said. "This party is going great! Everyone is having a great time. I was watching you across the fire, and you should have seen the smile on your face. You look so happy."

"You were watching me across the fire," Ethan put Jalyn on the spot with a twinkle in his eye.

"Yes, no, I don't know. Stop it! You know what I mean!" She couldn't help but blush.

Ethan grabbed her by the hand and guided her to the fire. By this time of the night, only a few people were left. Maddie joined them as they sat down.

Ethan was taking in this entire evening when he felt the need to talk to Maddie and Jalyn. "You know my life was a mess before, and I was not a nice person. I had been going to the brook walk for years to clear my head. All of a sudden I ran into you two, and you each changed me in a great way. I know this is a little much, but I owe you two everything. You took notice of me and talked to me. Like really talked to me. I guess, what I am trying to say is, thanks???"

Jalyn and Maddie looked at each other and back at Ethan with a smile. Maddie was the first to speak up. "Ethan, dude, you did this on your own. No one can change you; you have to change yourself. Gee, don't I sound philosophical!? Ha! Anyway, you, and your mom were the ones who changed my life. I was a mess that day I saw you at the brook walk, and the day I yelled at you, Jalyn, in tutoring. I was hiding from my life because I didn't want to be any part of it. I was drinking a lot and I felt lost and hopeless. You guys helped me figure out that cooking can be my future, and that is huge. At least for me, it was."

"Maybe it's the smores talking, but I feel the same way," Jalyn shared. "Ethan, and even you Maddie, helped me figure out who I wanted to be. I am not there yet, but I am working on it, and I am further along than I was before. That's what I call progress!"

They cheered, their smiles together, and Ethan said, "Here's to being happy!"

"No, here's to finding ticity!" Jalyn added.

"Ticity?" Maddie and Ethan said at the same time.

"Yes, ticity. It's a new word I made up. It works in this situation. Ticity is a feeling. It's a feeling of peace when you are truly being yourself. When you are living your life and following the path you are meant to be on. The outside world is not pulling you in artificial ways. You are content with where you are and who you are with," she smiled at Ethan and Maddie. "For me, there is a spiritual side to the word, but it doesn't have to be spiritual to you. It comes from authenticity. Like it? I am pretty proud of it."

"Well, there you have it," Ethan raised his mushy, dripping smores, "to ticity!"

"To ticity!" They all chimed in.

Maddie

Maddie was thinking about when she could barely focus on her drive home from Ethan's house that amazing Saturday afternoon. She had met with Mrs. Waltz to talk about a career in real estate, and ended up with what seemed to be the perfect career for her...cooking!

She could not wait until her parents came home from work that day. To keep herself busy, she cleaned the house and came up with an amazing dinner that night consisting of bacon ranch pasta with pesto topped garlic bread, added salad, and it sounded amazing. Something about all of that just felt right.

Finally, Maddie's efforts to clean the day away worked; it was 5 o'clock and in walked her parents.

Maddie smiled as she remembered greeting her parents. "Mama, Papa, welcome home!" Maddie danced around the room.

"So, Maddie, I take it that your meeting today went well?" Dad guessed.

"Never mind that. Look at this house, and something smells amazing!" Mom added.

"Yes, yes, and yes! I have been waiting all day to talk to you, but first, get ready for dinner. I made something special for you tonight!"

"You always make something special, Maddie. Let us change, and we will be right down," Mom said.

Maddie sat with her parents, chatting and enjoying the dinner she made. About two spoonfuls into the dinner, her dad chimed in, "Soooo, tell us what happened? Are you a future real estate agent?"

"Oh my gosh, I don't even know where to begin. I was talking to Ethan and his mom about real estate, which sounded like a great job. Lots of people interactions...a cool work environment...it was all good. But anyway, I had made them some of my brownies, and they couldn't stop talking about them. Ethan brought up my Maddiecakes, one thing led to another, and Mrs. Waltz started telling me about some great programs in the culinary arts. Cooking! Cooking! I can be a chef! Mom, can you believe it. You told me to find my superpower, and I truly think my superpower is cooking! What do you think?"

Maddie was a nervous mess. She knew in her heart of hearts that what she said was her truth, but she still cared a great deal about what her parents thought. She knew they wanted her to get a traditional bachelor's degree, but they had agreed to see where this journey led her. They accepted her for who she was, and always helped to make her the best version of herself. No matter what they said, she knew she would be successful with them by her side.

"Maddie, my word, I love that. You're right. Your superpower is something you can do better than most, and you definitely make one mean bacon ranch pasta dish!" Mom laughed.

"It's not going to be easy and any path you take will have challenges. I just have to say it again, you know having a bachelor's degree is going to help in any situation, right? In today's world, not having a degree puts you behind in most situations," Dad slowed himself down, "But that being said, you know we will be here for you." He leaned over and hugged Maddie. "This is your future, and it's your path. I am really proud of you for taking the initiative to research options and taking action to figure out your future. I have no doubt you will be great at anything you want to do. I do have to say that I will miss watching you play softball though. I guess I am going to have to soak up the next two seasons!"

"Speaking of softball, Maddie. I know you have taken a break from your coach to figure all of this out. Your dad and I were thinking that maybe we should cancel him for good. Let you play softball the way you always have, and just enjoy your time with the girls and your school coach. How does that sound?" Mom asked.

"I'm good with that. Playing softball for fun...it sounds too good to be true!" Maddie could almost see the weight she was so used to carrying on her chest vanish into thin air for good. All that stress, all that pressure, gone. She felt like she was living in a different world than just a few months ago. She knew the future was anything but guaranteed, but she felt more confident facing the future standing on her own two feet in a career that she felt she could totally rock.

"Maddie, how about after dinner, I pour a glass of wine, and we go on your laptop to find out more about these culinary arts programs. Oh, and if you ever need help with your cooking homework, I am your girl!"

"Thanks, Mom. Sounds good," Maddie laughed.

So Maddie and her mom cuddled up on the porch. Her mom with her favorite glass of cabernet, and Maddie with hot tea.

"So Mrs. Waltz talked about Westwood Area Junior College's program. She said it is pretty good. Maybe we should start there." Maddie entered the info and pulled up the website.

"Welcome to Westwood Area Junior College's first-class educational culinary arts program. WAJC's program has received many awards and national recognition

with many former students going on to open their own restaurants, managing kitchens around the world, and even starring in cooking shows on TV."

"Wow, who knew there were all these options!? You can focus on culinary arts, or just bread and pastries. Oh, maybe you should study desserts and cookies!" Maddie could see the excitement brewing her mom's eyes. She felt the same excitement inside of her.

"This is awesome. Look here. Look at all the cool events that students get to cook for!" Maddie was ready to sign up now! With each picture of the delicious meals that students had prepared, combined with the picture of a classroom full of students in white coats and hats, Maddie's mind was solidified in the fact that this was the right path for her. She could picture herself right in the middle of the classroom with absolutely no tutors in the picture. She truly never thought this would be a possibility, but here it was!

Her mom could sense the excitement her daughter was feeling. "Oh, Maddie, I am just bursting with happiness for you. This is really an amazing idea and exciting path for you. I am just busting with pride. You are my brave girl. I love you so much!"

"I am beyond excited! Wait, mom, look. They offer evening cooking classes for the general public. The classes are run by current students. Should I take one? Could I? Look at all these options! The classes are not too expensive. They have a technical cooking class that even starts next week, and it is not full yet!"

"Yes, go for it. Let's sign you up now. Wait, weren't you supposed to go hang out with your friends at Rob's house tonight? What time is that?"

"No, I don't think I am going to go tonight. Mom, how about we make popcorn and watch a movie here?"

Maddie could tell her mom was surprised by this response. "Absolutely. Great idea. Let's finish signing you up for this class, then we can head in."

Maddie snapped back into reality. The high of the weekend settled into the normalcy of the week. Even though Maddie was excited about her post-high school plans, she knew she still had a lot of high school left to get through. Maddie continued to meet with Jalyn for tutoring. She had even taken over tutoring Maddie in all her subjects. Jalyn seemed to have more time open, and Maddie really enjoyed this new, calmer Jalyn. She actually had quite a good sense of humor too. Softball pre-season would be starting soon, and Maddie could not wait to get started. Even though the extra coaching sessions had felt like so much work, she did truly love playing softball. She loved standing on the pitcher's mound, leading her team to victory.

When the day finally came for Maddie's cooking class, she pulled up a map of the school and wandered the hallways until she found the classroom. And what a classroom it was...ovens, utensils, stainless steel...everything. Maddie had to take a deep breath to make room for the all excitement building inside. Some people had already arrived, and there were people of all ages that came to take the class. They would be learning how to be more technical in the classroom with proper techniques in how to sear and sauté. Maddie couldn't wait to begin.

CHAPTER 9

Jalyn

"Soooo, are you excited?" Jalyn's dad had asked her while he poured his coffee one Saturday morning. "Aren't class officer elections coming up soon. I know this is always one of your favorite times of the year."

It's true. Jalyn always loved running for an officer position. She knew it was probably odd, but the thrill of making campaign posters, talking with people to secure votes, competing in debates, and then waiting with her heart pounding to hear the results being read over the morning announcements...there was something so thrilling about that process. Jalyn realized that she may have loved the adrenaline and anticipation of the unknown versus the actual process of being a class officer.

"Yeah, Dad. It's coming up soon." There was nothing else Jalyn could really say about that. She was still torn about going to the writing awards ceremony and expo. Why did the awards ceremony have to be the same time as class elections? It wasn't like she was completely against running as class president, but ugh, she wanted to go to the ceremony with all her heart. All she knew was that this sucked. Her family would be more disappointed than her if she skipped elections. There would certainly be a lot of surprised people at school.

Her dad broke into her thoughts. "Well, you should start thinking of your big campaign idea. Let me know if you need some help. I'm sure I can come up with some real winners for you!" He smirked and gave her a pat on the back.

As she headed back up to her room, Jalyn figured she should start brainstorming some campaign ideas. "Why not? It's not like I have anything else to do."

Once she was in her room, she fell backward onto her beanbag chair and closed her eyes. She could not see a solution to her problem. There was no way to be at two places at once. Again, the words of her grandpa came rushing back to her. "Give your struggles to God. Let Him in, and He can guide you."

It had become much easier for Jalyn to quiet her mind and find her place of prayer.

"God, I need to decide on a campaign idea for class officers next year. What should I do?" Jalyn asked knowing this wasn't really what she wanted to talk about. "Well, actually, God, I am torn. My life feels so much more on track now-a-days, but I am still torn. How much of my old life, and what part of my new life, am I supposed to embrace? There is so much of me still at odds with each other. I know You know the way. Please show it to me. I don't want to upset my family. They have so many hopes for me, and they are good hopes. I just don't think they are my goals anymore. Maybe they never were my goals? I can't go to the competition, can I? There is no point in even telling them about the event. It's the same time as the debates. It won't work," Jalyn was torn by her response. Jalyn could feel her thoughts pulling from the inside. "What do you really want to do?" She just sat there and thought. "Next year is my senior year, what do I want it to look like. What will make me happy with myself? Not what others want, but truly think about what I want." Jalyn knew there was no sense in disagreeing with her thoughts.

So Jalyn closed her eyes, quieted her mind, and just sat in peace. After about 20 minutes of silence, Jalyn grabbed her list from under her mattress, and out fell the awards ceremony invite. She decided to just make a list on that piece of paper. On one side she would put down things she wanted to do next year, and on the other side, she would put down things she didn't want to do. She put everyone else out of her mind, and just focused on herself. "Don't think about it, just write the list now."

Jalyn started to write a list titled: Keep and Quit. Keep: workouts, writing, helping others/tutoring, working hard at school. Quit: Viola and... class officers?

Jalyn could barely believe she had written that down on paper. She had been ignoring her thoughts about this for a while now. But she knew it was true. She enjoyed being a class officer, but it took up a ton of time. A ton of time she could use to write or hang out with friends. It took Jalyn a minute to realize that this was as real as she could be. She was changing, and she could no longer fight it. "Being a class officer had always been a source of pride for me. But if I am being honest, it also gives me these long to-do lists and stress. It just doesn't feel like me anymore. That's my truth."

Jalyn knew this was the truth. She had been losing interest in her to-do lists, and instead enjoyed writing and hanging out with friends. She also knew that she wanted to go to the awards ceremony. This also meant upsetting her parents, but there was no way around that. She knew her grandpa would help her, and maybe he was right; her parents loved her, and they would eventually come around, wouldn't they?

There had also been this one thing she had been toying with in her mind. She was thinking about starting a Writing Club at school. There are no clubs for writers, and she thought it would be awesome to get people together to plan and create story ideas. It would be amazing if that would work. She loved the time she spent sharing ideas with Mrs. Ozark, but she bet there were other inspiring writers out there. Imagine if they could all come together and share ideas. On the other hand, the club was such a far-fetched idea. She has never started a club before, and she was a little nervous to bring the idea up. Jalyn was excited that she had finally let her nagging idea see the light of day. She added it to her Keep List.

"In fact," and this was definitely something Jalyn had not said out loud to anyone yet, "I was thinking it would be awesome to help Ethan run for class president. I think he would be so good at it. He really seems to love all the work that comes from the position. Oh, my, this is crazy! What will he think? Maybe I could be his campaign manager!" Of course she agreed with herself since no one was there to listen.

Jalyn was absolutely glowing at this point. She was alive with exciting new ideas.

All of this was true, so true. Jalyn loved the idea of being behind the scenes. She could be who she wanted to be, and now it was clear to her what she needed to do. All she had left to do was tell her parents!

Jalyn grabbed her phone and called her grandpa. "Hey, Grandpa! I really need to talk to you. Can you stop over whenever you get some time?"

"Of course, Jalyn. I have some time open this afternoon. See you soon!"

Ethan

Jalyn came running into school the next day, barreling toward Ethan. She was exceptionally excited to see him, but even Ethan knew something must be up.

"What's going on?" Ethan asked. "You are, ummm, quite hyper this morning."

"I have the best idea ever invented, ever imagined, ever created! Jalyn looked like she would explode if she didn't get this information out soon.

Even though he was a little overwhelmed, he said, "I'm all ears," and Ethan waited eagerly.

"You, Ethan Waltz, are going to run for...wait for it...wait for it...class president!!"

She sat back, breathing heavy, eyes popping with anticipation. He knew she was waiting for him to get excited, but he was so confused. She must be losing her mind! "Isn't that your goal? Isn't that what you have been wanting for, for like ever?" Ethan didn't hate the idea, but he would never take this away from Jalyn. Everyone at the school knew who the senior class president would be. Oh, sure, there were other candidates, and they were great, and in other schools, they would probably win, but she was Jalyn Chibuzo. I mean, come on.

"I thought it was, but it's really not. It's truly not something I want anymore. Kind of surprised myself with that one too, not gonna lie," Jalyn said as she got a little closer to Ethan and whispered. "It's true. I know it is hard to understand, but you have to trust me. I have been thinking and praying about this a lot. Oh, Ethan, so much has changed, in such a good way. I know this is all so crazy, but it's the right thing to do. I know you feel it too."

Ethan stood there quite uncertain how to exactly respond to Jalyn. The idea completely freaked him out, but something about it just sounded amazing. He didn't even know if it could even be done.

"But how would I even," before Ethan could finish his sentence, Jalyn interrupted, "I will be your campaign manager. Come on! You were made for this job. You are such a great leader. Look around, Ethan, you have changed so much this year. Everyone in these hallways knows it. They can see it. I know how to win a campaign. I guess all that really matters is - Is this something you truly want to do?"

"Would you still run for an officer position? I mean another officer position? I mean...I don't know if I could do this on my own?" Ethan stumbled over his words. It's true that Ethan had earned so many new friends, and people did truly seem to like him and want to be around him. All he had to do was be himself, nothing more. But Jalyn was always doing so much for the school. There was a ton of work to be done as a class officer. Was Ethan really prepared to take this on?

"No, I wouldn't run for any office. I actually have some other projects up my sleeve that I want to focus on instead. I won't have time to do everything that is needed to be an officer, but I will always be there to help you. Just like you helped me this year."

Jalyn was beaming with excitement, but Ethan's mind was spinning. It's true, he had worked really hard this year to change his life and reputation. He had gone out of his comfort zone and become a part of his school, a part of his own life. He liked getting to know his classmates, and people seemed to respond to him. Sometimes he still wondered if they responded so positively to him because they liked him or were they still afraid of him. Maybe he would never really know, but running for class president was a whole new territory. Something about it just felt right. He would have to put himself out there, and he would be at the mercy of his classmates' judgment. All he could do was take a risk and hope for the best. This was the way he had spent most of the year anyway. If Jalyn thought it was a good idea, then maybe it wasn't the worst idea ever.

"Ok," he said and looked at Jalyn, "Let's do this!"

Once Ethan decided to run, Jalyn hit fast forward on his campaign. She was in a league of her own as far as planning and organizing everything to do with class officers, and Ethan knew she was out of his league! The process of running for a class officer was like a leap of faith. Candidates put themselves out there, let people know what they stood for, and just waited to see what happened.

Ethan was a natural though. Throughout the campaign process, Jalyn could see it. Ethan had such an ease about him talking to people and promoting his campaign. He was honest and straightforward. He did not have the same insecurities Jalyn always had worrying if people were going to like her. Ethan did not worry about whether or not people liked him. He just wondered if people would accept him. These past months had been a rehaul of his life, and while he really enjoyed this Ethan 2.0 version, it did seem as if people were accepting him for the changes he was making.

Throughout the campaign, Jalyn was by Ethan's side, and man, she had some great ideas. But more than that, Ethan was realizing his feelings for Jalyn were growing stronger. He loved her laugh, the way she chewed on her long hair when she was brainstorming ideas, and the light in her eyes when she came up with just the right idea or just the right word for a situation.

He tried to think back to the days when Jalyn was merely a means to an end. She was smart, and he needed her homework. He always thought she was pretty, but now he just loved the person she was on the inside and the friend she had become to him. He did not know if he would be the person he was today without her.

But therein laid the problem. Ethan had gotten so good at letting people in and taking an interest in others, but he had yet to fully let Jalyn know how he felt. He was afraid she wouldn't feel the same way. Then everything good between them would be changed. His mom had been asking him relentlessly if he liked Jalyn, and he kept telling her that they were awesome as friends, nothing more. He knew that she knew, he was lying. She was coming over soon to help make more posters and work on his campaign speech. Maybe he could tell her how he felt tonight?

It was still early in the process, and Jalyn had not told her parents she wasn't running for president. Every time they got together to work on the campaign, Jalyn told her parents it was for her. Ethan wished he could help her with this, but he figured it was something she had to figure out on her own with her parents. Just then the doorbell rang, and Ethan jumped up to greet Jalyn at the door.

"Hey!" Ethan greeted.

"Hey, yourself!" Man, that smile made Ethan's heart skip a beat. "Are you ready for some fun? I brought posters, markers, and lots of ideas for a campaign speech."

"Wow, aren't you a party in a box!" Ethan said with extra enthusiasm. He knew teasing Jalyn about her nerdiness always made her laugh. She loved this kind of stuff.

"Shut up! Or I am walking right out that door and running against you in this campaign! I wonder who would win then?" Jalyn looked at him with her hands on her hips and eyes all aglow.

"Uncle, uncle, I give...you win! I would love to party "campaign-style" with you. Anyone who watched the two of them could easily see their connection, and it did not take much to recognize the flirting that was going on between them.

Over the next two hours, Ethan and Jalyn brainstormed, laughed, and shared ideas. Their conversations flowed with such ease, and there was a magnetic attraction that pulled them together. Neither of them wanted the evening to end.

Ethan still had not told Jalyn anything about his feelings, and he had absolutely no idea how to even begin. They both had been going through so much lately, and their visits to the pond were a regular part of their friendship. Ethan figured Jalyn had to know how he felt, right? They spent so much time together. How could she not know?

"Jalyn, do you know how much I appreciate all you have done to help me? I mean...none of this would even be happening if you hadn't seen something in me. I am not sure you know how I feel about you..."

"Aww, aren't you just the sweetest!" Jalyn reached over and hugged Ethan. "You are pretty cool yourself...well, most of the time!" She laughed and popped up to leave.

"No..." Ethan said in his head. They spent so much of their time joking and teasing that she did not realize he was trying to be serious.

Jalyn gathered her stuff, popped her head in to say bye to his mom, and started for the door. "I'll see you tomorrow, Mr. President." She waved and headed out the door.

Defeated, Ethan sat back in his room looking through his campaign speech. All in all, he liked the speech and talking points for the debates. His number one goal was just to be himself and see what happens. Winning or losing wasn't really stressing him out. It was more just the process that he enjoyed. He liked being part of something positive.

"Hey, Ethan. How did it go with Jalyn?" His mom peeked her head around the corner.

"Great, really great. She knows her stuff and she has a ton of amazing ideas. I am totally digging this campaign stuff, Mom. How shocking is that?"

"Shocking indeed. You know," she inched further into his room. "Your dad called again today. Do you want to call him back? I don't care what you do, but he did sound like he really wanted to talk with you."

Ethan had no real response. It's not that he never wanted to see his dad again, but he had been working so hard to peel away his likeness to his dad. He was not sure he was ready to see him yet. "Mom, I think I just need more time. Right now I just want to focus on my life. I am not going to ignore him forever, but for right now, I am."

"Hey, I support you. It's all good. Do you mind just texting him back and telling him you're busy so he stops calling? He will always be your dad, and I will never get in the way of that, but I can certainly do with fewer calls from him," his mom laughed and shut the door.

Texting! Yes, that was it...maybe Ethan could text Jalyn and let her know how he felt? Nah, that was stupid. What about a letter? Jalyn loved writing, maybe Ethan could write to her.

An hour later, Ethan sat surrounded by a pile of crumpled papers, no closer to telling Jalyn how he felt.

Maddie

The cooking instructor was a lady that Maddie guessed was in her 20s, but she reminded Maddie of her favorite aunt with a bright smile and welcoming eyes. After a round of get-to-know-you questions, the instructor asked everyone to grab a seat around the table. She informed the group that she would be demonstrating the skills first, then they would partner up by one of the stovetops, and practice the skills. Best part...they got to eat their classwork in the end!

Maddie soaked up every bit of instruction and loved every minute of class, which was not something she had ever thought she could feel. They learned how to sear meat to create a mouth-watering flavor, and sauté by making sure the pan was hot enough to brown meat or vegetables. They were to test the heat of the pan by splashing a drop of water into the pan, if it sizzles and turns to steam immediately, it's ready.

When it was time to partner up, Maddie looked around the room and caught the eye of a guy near her. She smiled as he said, "Want to partner up?"

"Sure. Hi, I'm Keith."

"Nice to meet you, my name's Maddie. Is this your first cooking class?"

"No, third actually. I work for the college, so I get to take classes at a reduced rate. I am getting married in the fall, so I figured why not learn how to cook. Well, at least how to cook with something other than the microwave."

They laughed.

"How many classes have you taken?" Keith asked.

"This is my first."

"Ah, well, welcome. You'll like this class. She is a great teacher."

"Awesome."

Keith and Maddie put on the provided apron and head covering, set up the utensils, and organized their food.

"So what made you want to take a cooking class? We do not get many high school students in here?" Keith asked.

"Well, I am actually thinking of going to college for culinary arts after high school, and I love to cook. I was looking at the school's website and saw this class, figured I would give it a try," Maddie answered.

"Nice! We have a great program here at WAJC. I actually work as a dean here at the school, so if you have any questions, just let me know."

"Thanks!" Maddie said and turned her focus to the class and the teacher. For the first time, Maddie did not want to waste one minute of school.

Maddie was a "natural" at searing and sautéing, or at least that is what the teacher said. Maddie was beaming with pride and loving the positive feedback she was getting from the instructor. She had never been the star pupil before and based on how her food turned out, school had never been so delicious. The class was two hours of pure bliss.

Keith offered to show her around the campus after the class, and Maddie was quick to take him up on the offer. Her friends were starting to go on college visits, maybe she should too.

He showed her around the classrooms, outside study area, library, the performing arts center, computer lab, fitness center, and then the outdoor athletic facilities.

"No way! That's a softball field!!??!" Maddie burst out making Keith jump back a bit.

"Ah, yes, we have a softball team. WAJC has a great softball program. The Rockets softball team has won the NJCAA national championship for the past two years. I take it you play?"

"Play? Yes! I absolutely love the sport. My parents and coaches want me to go to college and try for a softball scholarship, but college is not really my thing." She caught herself. "I mean this college is my thing, I think... just not, you know, a four-year college. I want to become a chef. But I love softball just as much as cooking!"

"I get what you mean about a four-year degree program. Traditional school is not for everyone. We have some top-notch associate's degree and certification programs here. I think you will find that there are many students studying a wide variety of careers here at WAJC. I know making big decisions about your future can be scary, no matter what you decide to do. Sometimes you just have to trust your instincts and take a leap of faith," Keith explained. "And, it sounds like you are someone our coach should know about. He's not on campus now, they start practice in about a week, but I will be sure to pass your name along. Do you go to Westwood High School?"

"Yes. That would be awesome. Thank you so much, Keith. I should probably call you, Mr. umm, what's your last name?" Maddie suddenly realized she was talking to the dean for her potential school and not a classmate in a cooking class.

He laughed, "My last name is Richards, but you can call me Keith. Most of the students do too. Alright, so that about concludes the grand tour. It was great meeting you Maddie. I can walk you back to where your car is located."

"Thank you for everything. It was great meeting you too. If you don't mind, I would like to wander around a little more on my own."

"No problem at all! See you in the next cooking class. Oh, and I'll be sure to pass along your information to Coach Balister. Take care." Keith waved goodbye.

"Bye. Thanks again for everything," Maddie responded.

Maddie spent the next hour wandering around the campus, taking pictures to go back and show her parents.

As she unlocked her car, she couldn't help but feel that she was unlocking her future. Any doubts she had before, seemed to melt away.

Later that night, she told her parents all about the class, the cooking, the teacher's praise, meeting the dean, and of course the softball team. The pictures on her phone helped show the story of what she experienced that day. She could tell her parents were feeling the same way she did about her future.

"Maddie, I am impressed with all the work you have done to learn about this new career idea. Maybe we should set up a tour of the junior college and probably some other places that have culinary arts programs. You want to make sure you know all your options before you decide," Dad said. "Did you ever meet with your guidance counselor to talk to her about your options?"

Maddie had completely forgotten about her appointment with the guidance counselor the next week. "Actually, I have an appointment next week."

"Great, sounds like you have a plan."

CHAPTER 10

Jalyn

As soon as Jalyn walked into English class, Mrs. Ozark called her over to her desk. She knew Mrs. Ozark would ask her about the competition awards.

"So, any word on whether or not you can attend the awards?" It was obvious to Jalyn that Mrs. Ozark was proud of the writer she had helped discover, and Jalyn did not want to let her down. But the truth was that her parents still did not know that Jalyn had won an award, and with it being the same time as officer debates, well, Jalyn had not gotten up the nerve to talk to them. They did not even know yet that she was not planning on running for class officer. She hadn't been quite brave enough to share the whole truth about the situation. But the clock was ticking, and she would have to do something fast. The RSVP deadline for the awards ceremony was this week. This was also the last week to get candidates registered for the class officer campaign, so her parents would eventually know her name was not on the list. Her grandpa had given her a pep talk too when he stopped over the other day. But no pep talk in the world could ultimately prepare Jalyn for what she knew she had to do.

"I'm still waiting to hear...scheduling and all. I know I have to respond soon. I will talk with them tonight and find out for sure," Jalyn gathered some strength to ask the question she was really wondering. "Mrs. Ozark, I really love writing. It has meant the world to me and changed me in so many ways, but...it's just...my parents...I was wondering..." she tried with all she could to get the words out. "Could I really do this for a living? Am I just wasting my time? Is writing just a hobby or a job skill? College is right around the corner, and I thought I wanted to be a pediatrician, but now I am not so sure. But my parents will freak because, well, a doctor is a doctor, and a writer...it just sounds like a more uncertain path. What do you think?" Jalyn knew all of these words came spilling out in a pile on Mrs. Ozark's desk, and there was a good chance Jalyn had offended her teacher.

Mrs. Ozark had a look of pride and determination in her eyes. "Jalyn, deciding on your future is not an easy thing to do, for anyone, especially at your age. It's great that you are thinking about all of this now. All I know is that if you find a job doing what you love, what you were meant to do, well, that makes this whole work thing a lot easier. There are amazing career opportunities out there for writers, and outstanding colleges with excellent writing and journalism degrees. The field of writing is vast. You can do a hundred different jobs as a writer across a hundred different fields. You have a natural talent as a writer, anyone could see that. I read some of the recent pieces you wrote, and they are excellent, really engaging. I can't tell you what you should do, but if you want to pursue a career in writing, I can promise you that there are opportunities out there for people with your talents."

This was exactly what Jalyn needed to hear to give her the boost she needed to finally have a conversation with her parents, even though she knew it was not going to be easy.

"Thanks, Mrs. Ozark. I'll let you know about the competition awards tomorrow."

That night Jalyn's family piled into the car on their way to Fresco's for dinner with her grandparents. As the minutes passed by, Jalyn could feel her chances of talking to her parents slipping away. She could hear the words in her head, but she could not shove them out of her mouth. She would have to speak up soon or wait until after dinner to get this off her chest.

Finally, she just blurted out the words. "I am not going to run for class officer, and I want to quit viola. They take up too much time." Once she opened the floodgates, the truth came pouring out. "I want to help Ethan run for class president. He will be so good at the job. And I really want to go to the writing competition awards. Oh, by the way, my story won third place in the competition - that's the good news! I have been writing a lot lately, and Mrs. Ozark likes my work. She thinks I can be a writer - like as a profession. And I want to start a writing club for other students, and...that's it."

She knew she had just dropped a bomb of atomic proportions in that car. Although she had been living with this truth for quite some time, this was the first her parents were hearing of it. They were already concerned about the changes they had been seeing in Jalyn, and this certainly was not going to help.

Her dad pulled the car over on the side of the road, and that was never a good thing! Her parents just looked at each other without saying a word.

"I knew hanging out with that Ethan kid was going to drag you down. Did he put you up to this?" her mom asked.

"You always wanted to be a pediatrician. You need leadership positions at school and musical instrument experience to make it into a top school. If you quit them, what are you going to do?" her dad pounded, just as concerned. "Why are you throwing your future away? We all work in the medical field. It has served us well, and it is a respected profession to follow. All of this is coming out of nowhere. You are throwing your future away and for what? A story award and opportunity to write? What are you going to do as a writer? Do you know how many people are writers? Not many.

You are too smart for that. With your brains and drive, you can do so much better. We expect you to do so much better!"

"But it's my future, mine!" Jalyn could feel she was losing her cool, but she didn't care. "This is my life. I have my own expectations for myself." Even saying these words made Jalyn realize that this was the truth. She had no idea if she ever really wanted to be a pediatrician or was it just something she was supposed to do. She had never before known what her own self expectations had been, but now she did. And maybe it was a mistake, but it was her mistake to make.

"I want to be a writer. I really do," Jalyn said, calmer now. She could see that they had arrived at the restaurant and were pulling into the parking lot.

"Jalyn, let's table this for now. I don't want to hear a word about this at dinner. This whole discussion will upset your grandparents."

She barely spoke the entire dinner. Jalyn kept running the conversation over and over in her mind. But one thing remained clear, she knew she was making the right decision for herself. Her grandfather noticed that Jalyn was quite distant during dinner, and finally asked, "Jalyn, you seem quiet tonight. Are you okay?"

She looked at her mom who was shooting her a look that clearly said to keep quiet, so Jalyn obeyed. "I'm fine. Just tired."

As soon as those words left her mouth, she knew they were not at all true. She wasn't fine, she wanted to be fine, but she wasn't, and her grandpa correctly guessed what had happened.

"Jalyn, I don't think you are fine. Tell us what's going on." Grandpa asked fully knowing what she was going to say.

"Not now, Dad. This is not the time or the place." Jalyn's dad directed.

But Jalyn could see the prodding look in her grandfather's eyes, so she started without making eye contact with her parents. "I've decided that I want to be a writer and not a pediatrician. I guess that is upsetting everyone. I don't want to work in the medical field."

Her grandfather looked over at her parents, gave a small smirk, and asked, "Well, that doesn't sound like bad news? It actually sounds quite interesting! Tell me more about it." Her grandma did not seem too convinced.

Jalyn was not sure what to do, so she focused on her grandpa.

Instead of defending herself, she gathered herself instead, and shared, what she thought, was some amazing news. "Well, I have been doing a lot of writing. I think it is pretty good. At least my English teacher thinks so, and she said my stories were well written. She thinks I have a unique talent and that I could make a career as a writer. I wrote a narrative story and it came in third place in the category of young adult short stories in the Stenitzer National Writing Award competition. There is a big award ceremony coming up in California, and I was invited to attend. I have to respond by this week to reserve a spot for me and my guests. I have been writing a lot lately, and I love every minute of it. Mrs. Ozark said that there are many college programs with strong writing degree programs. It seems like an exciting field to study." Jalyn paused. This was the stinger part. "I have also decided I don't want to be a class officer, and I want to give up the viola. This will give me more time to focus on what I am truly interested in for the future." Jalyn sat back. Well, there it was, all of it, out in the open. There was no turning back now, and Jalyn knew it. Obviously, there was more to these changes than she shared, but some things were private.

At that moment, her dad put his glass down hard on the table and everyone turned to look in his direction. No one spoke again for a while.

Finally, her grandfather jumped in, "Why don't you guys let me take Jalyn to California for the awards ceremony. I have an old friend who lives out that way, and it would be great to see him. It's been years."

"Dad, not now, please." Jalyn's father wanted nothing to do with this. In reality, this conversation didn't upset Jalyn's grandparents as much as it upset her parents.

The rest of the dinner passed in silence. Jalyn felt terrible about upsetting her parents, but she felt so free because her truth and her path were in the open.

At one point she caught her grandpa's eye and mouthed, "Thank you." He winked back and smiled.

After they paid for the check, Grandma kept Jalyn and her mom back at the table while Grandpa asked to talk to Dad outside. Jalyn's grandmother was a natural at starting conversations and got Jalyn's mom talking about her job and recent shopping trips. Jalyn was thankful that the focus was off her for a while but eager to know what was happening outside.

On the car ride home, silence was playing on repeat, and it wasn't until the next day that Jalyn's parent's sat down to talk to her.

"Before you begin, I want you to know that none of this was meant to hurt you. The last thing I wanted to do was disappoint you. Heck, I have spent my life making sure I did not disappoint you. But I realized that I wasn't being true to myself. I am sorry." Her parents looked at her, looked at each other, and started talking.

It turns out that somehow her grandfather had convinced her parents to let her go to the awards ceremony as long as Grandpa went with Jalyn. They also said she could make her own decisions about her school activities. Jalyn felt they were doing it more to help teach her a lesson, but it all just felt so right. As Jalyn sat looking at her to-be list, she knew she had done everything she could to align her life to what she wanted it to look like.

Before leaving for the trip, she had gone to the principal and presented a proposal about starting a writing club. Jalyn had set up an information booth during lunches and talked to so many students who were also interested in writing. She had never imagined there were so many different people who enjoyed writing. Some of her classmates enjoyed writing poetry, some political pieces. She loved the diversity of interests and could not wait to get started.

The rest of her time before the trip was spent helping Ethan on his campaign. He was officially running for class officer, and even though she knew it was going to take a lot to get him elected, she knew in her heart that he was the right person for the job.

"I can't believe the debates and the election are almost here!" Jalyn said to Ethan as they were sitting by the pond one day after school. This place had become their escape, their place of peace.

"And I can't believe you aren't going to be there! Are your parents any better with the whole awards competition?" Ethan asked.

"You know, it ultimately doesn't matter, but they seem to be, I guess. But I am beyond excited, and I am so glad my grandpa is going with me. He seems excited too. There are so many speakers, exhibits, and writing workshops to attend. I bought a new fancy dress for the awards ceremony and all! Uh, I just can't wait! But don't worry, I ask the principal if I could cast my vote for class officers before I leave. If only I could decide who to vote for?? Hmmmm, let's see, there is that Peter boy. He seems pretty reliable. Haha!" Jalyn threw herself back onto the blanket and laughed.

"You are so funny...you know that!" Ethan laid back beside Jalyn. She could feel Ethan's hand against her own. She wanted badly to grab it. This spark, this feeling she had with Ethan was unlike anything she had felt before. Nothing in the world existed at this moment aside from the two of them in a field of flowers next to a calm, still pond. She just wondered if Ethan felt the way she did?

Ethan

Ethan felt time stand still. Jalyn was right next to him. Her hand touched his. He never did find the guts to tell Jalyn how he felt, but at this moment it did not seem to matter. Everything was perfect, and he could feel the magic between them. It was as if there was something in the air between them drawing them close. Ethan reached a little further and grabbed Jalyn's hand in his own. He turned to look at this amazing person next to him, just as she was turning to look at him. They leaned their heads in closer, and he leaned over and kissed her. Nothing had been more perfect in his entire life. She returned the kiss with her soft sweet lips. They laid together kissing, not saying a word. Everything had already been said.

The memory of their first kiss embraced Ethan's mind for the next few days, mostly because Jalyn had left for her trip and he wouldn't see her for a few days. He worked hard to put his thoughts of Jalyn aside and focus on the debates. His mom had helped him rehearse all last night, and Maddie had promised Jalyn she would be there by his side to cheer him on.

He kept remembering what his mom had said to him the other day. "I knew from the beginning that you were going to like the real person inside of you. It was a journey to get here, but I know it was worth it. I'm proud of you, son."

All Ethan could do was smile. It was true. He sat behind the podium a completely different person compared to who he had been at the beginning of the school year.

He started the school year as an angry, unhappy person. He used everyone around him and got close to no one. He flinched at the thought of who he had been, and especially how he had treated his mom. He pushed this image of the old him out of his mind and focused on who he had become instead. Thanks to his mom, Jalyn, and even his dad, he had changed everything. He was no longer angry at the world. By working to understand the people around him, he was able to let this side of himself go. And now, sitting here, running for class president, he was helping those around him learn more about who he was as a person.

"Candidates you may now take your places." And so it began.

After the debates Maddie found Ethan "You did amazing! Ethan seriously! You were great. Did you text Jalyn? She has been texting me every 2 minutes. I figured you should be the one to tell her how it went." Maddie, along with other classmates, were congratulating the candidates after the debates.

It was true. Ethan had felt that the debate went great. He felt strong up there. He had opinions and perspectives, and he was very comfortable sharing them. Throughout the campaign, he realized that he had made so many new friends, gained confidence in what he believed, and most importantly, convinced himself that he had truly changed for the better. He had really used this platform to show the school, and himself, who he was as a person and what he was capable of doing.

After school, Jalyn made Ethan give her a play-by-play of every sentence, argument, and point made in the debates. When she had finally gotten every detail she could out of him, she asked, "So are you nervous to get the results of the election?"

"You know, Jalyn, it doesn't really matter what happens at the election. I already feel like I have won." He could feel Jalyn smiling on the other end of the phone.

He had to rehash the entire conversation again that night to his mom at dinner. Ethan was so exhausted hearing his own voice, but there was no way his mom was going to let it settle at, "The debates went well." Just like Jalyn she had a million questions.

"How exciting. Order anything you want off the menu. I am dining with the president tonight, folks!" Ethan's mom said loud enough for others to hear.

Ethan was so embarrassed, "Mom, who knows if I will even win. I have to wait a few days to find out." But secretly he was thrilled at her reaction and thrilled at the prospect of winning.

"So, Ethan, there is something else I need to ask you." Mom paused. "Your dad asked if he could stop by tonight at the house and see you. I may or may not have mentioned the election, and he wanted to stop by and congratulate you."

This took Ethan by surprise, he knew he was going to have to talk to his dad again, he had just been putting it off. But he figured now was as good of a time as any.

"I guess. It's fine, Mom. You can tell him to come over."

After their royal feast, as Mom had called it, they returned home to find Ethan's dad waiting in the driveway.

"I'll see you inside, dear." Mom kissed Ethan on the forehead and headed inside.

"Hey."

"Hey."

"I think this is the first time I have ever waited for you to arrive?" Ethan's dad started the conversation.

"Ain't that the truth." Ethan couldn't help but bark back a little.

"So I heard you did some sort of speech today and that you are running for class president."

"Yep."

"Listen, son, I don't know what to say after our last conversation, but what I told you was the truth. I can't change the past, and I can't change me. Your mom always said she was afraid of you turning out like me, and well, I can't say I blame her. But clearly, you are your own man. Lord knows I would never do this president thing. So I guess I just wanted to tell you that I am proud of you. And I guess I am proud that you are a stronger man than I was."

Ethan was floored. He couldn't remember a time that his dad had actually focused on him for more than two seconds, let alone actually known details about Ethan's life, and complimented him.

"Life has a funny way of taking you for a ride, doesn't it?" Ethan said to his dad, but also just to the air as his explanation of the past school year.

"That it does, son. That it does. So I'd like us to meet again for lunch or dinner some time if we could. I think you are inspiring me to make some changes. Yes, yes indeed. Your old man is going to be making some positive changes in his life."

"Okay, Dad." Ethan knew that would never happen, but he guessed at the end of the day, any relationship with his dad was better than no relationship at all.

After his dad left, Ethan sat looking at the stars and reading Jalyn's last text.

"Heading home in the morning! Can't wait to see you...and kiss you ;)"

"I can't wait either," Ethan thought.

Maddie

Jalyn's reaction to Maddie's news about Westwood Area Junior College's culinary arts program and nationally-ranked softball team was almost too much to handle.

Maddie could not contain her laughter as she looked at Jalyn's eyes wide open filled with pure awe and discovery. "Jalyn, you look like you heard they discovered alien life. Junior colleges are colleges too, you know," Maddie teased.

"You're right. I guess I just never thought about it. Wow," she was still soaking it all in. "That is an amazing opportunity for someone who is not sure what they want to do for school or wants to do something other than a degree program. And you can play softball there too? Huh, that's pretty cool. I wonder if other people know about this."

Maddie rolled her eyes. She may be the one getting tutored, but Jalyn can certainly use to lift her head up once in a while and see how the rest of the world lives.

"You know, Jalyn, I am meeting with my guidance counselor this afternoon. I'll be sure to ask."

"Good idea!" Maddie laughed as her sarcasm flew right past Jalyn. "Anyway, how do you feel about your science test today? Do you want to review the chemical equations again? One more time for fun?"

Maddie fully understood Jalyn's sarcasm. "No, Ms. Tutor, I think I am good."

"Great. Hey, Ethan was thinking of having another s'mores night bonfire at his house after the election is over. I know you were Queen S'mores, so I hope you can make it."

"Wouldn't miss it for the world. Thanks, Jalyn. Bye."

Maddie's guidance counselor's name was Mrs. Carter. She was an all-business kind of person, with a very serious tone to everything she said. Maddie was always so intrigued and amused to talk with her because she really had never met anyone who was so serious all the time. Mrs. Carter was impressed with the work Maddie had done already to research culinary arts programs. She gave her some more information on other area programs that she may want to check out in the future. She reminded Maddie that most applications were due in the fall of her senior year, so they should meet again at that time.

"Great, thanks, Mrs. Carter," Maddie said as she was packing up to leave.

"Maddie, now that I am thinking about it, how would you like to speak at the school's career fair about your interest in the culinary arts and what you have experienced so far looking at WAJC?"

Maddie was floored, "But isn't a career fair for someone who has a, you know, career. What could I possibly talk about?" Maddie had never been big on class presentations.

"Don't be silly. Students can benefit from the college exploration you have already done. And a lot of kids don't realize the financial and academic benefits of attending a junior college. The Westwood Area Junior College has some exceptional programs. Maybe you can research the various programs at the school and include that in your presentation? What do you think?"

Maddie was honored to be asked and figured she probably could do the presentation with some help. "Sure, thank you for asking me. I'd love to do it."

"Great! Go home and talk with your parents. I will email you the presentation requirements."

Maddie found herself, once again, sharing some big news with her parents over dinner.

"Well isn't that something, Maddie. You should be feeling pretty good right about now." Maddie could tell her dad was starting to get on board with this no-college, college plan, and she was glad. Her mom volunteered to help her create the presentation, and they both said they would take the day off of work to come see it.

"Uh, my parents at school. I don't know that this is really an event for parents?" Maddie was grateful and all, but still!

"Oh, relax, we can blend in the background. The students will think we are there as Career Day presenters. No one will be the wiser."

Maddie guessed that sounded reasonable.

"There's so much work to do for this presentation. I have to start researching the various programs at the school. In fact, I started looking earlier, and there is a program to learn how to become a massage therapist."

"Nice! Maybe your dad can go back to school with you!" Maddie's mom exclaimed and leaned her hip into her husband. "A massage sounds wonderful!"

"Sure, no problem! I will just set up a massage business right here in the kitchen," he laughed and turned his attention back to Maddie. "When does softball start? I think you will have a pretty good team this year."

"Actually, the first day of softball is the same day at the Career Fair. So that should be an exciting day."

Maddie spent the next week preparing her presentation, changing her presentation, adding new information, and finally rehearsing it. Mrs. Carter had reviewed the content and given her final approval, so all Maddie had left to do was figure out what she would wear and practice, practice, practice.

When the day for the Career Fair finally arrived, Maddie walked into the gym, which was now transformed into aisles and aisles of displays. The last time she saw the gym this way was before freshman year when she walked the gym looking at all the different clubs and activities the school had to offer. She figured this was almost like that event except for instead of clubs and activities, it was jobs and careers...an activity fair for soon-to-be adults.

Maddie followed Mrs. Clark and went over to where she wanted her to set up, and Maddie was blown away. She was in a section with trades and vocational opportunities. There was a booth with Westwood firefighters and police officers, local hair stylists, and even an x-ray technician. If Maddie wasn't nervous before, she certainly was now. Her booth was called "Helping You Decide the Next Step."

"I can do this," Maddie thought. "She knew she could talk about what she was doing to decide the next step."

Before she knew it, the flood water of students started pouring in from every door. The gym was packed with professionals talking about their jobs and what it took to prepare for a career in their field. It took a while, but one-by-one students started coming over to her asking about her booth. She showed them her presentation and talked about her own experiences. Most were quite impressed. "Maddie, you are so much further along in all of this than I am. I have no clue what I am going to do."

"Well, I guess it's a good thing you can look through all these options today," Maddie said, and just out of the corner of her eye she spotted her parents. They were doing a good job of just blending in. Maddie's heart filled with joy. She was so lucky to always have the constant support of her parents. They never wavered or gave up on her.

Maddie smiled, waved, gave them a thumbs-up, and kept talking to the students. By now, more and more of them were coming up to talk to her. Word got out that her booth was "worth visiting," as one person said. Jalyn and Ethan even stopped over to say hi and listen to her presentation. "Thanks for coming over here!" Maddie had said.

"Of course! We are here to support you. It's the least I could do for all the help you gave me trying to keep me calm before the debates!" said Ethan with a big smile.

By the end of the fair, Maddie was talked out and ready to take off her dress shoes. "How does anyone work all day in these fancy clothes?"

Luckily, her next stop was the gym locker room to change into her softball practice clothes. "Now that feels more like it," she said to herself after she had changed and locked up her school book.

The locker room was a-buzz with all the spring sports starting up today. Maddie greeted her teammates, exchanged inside jokes, and pumped each other up for a great season. Finally, the coach pounded on the door, "Softball girls, let's go! I want you on the field in 5 minutes."

Maddie walked out to the field with her new spikes on her feet, softball bag on her shoulders, perfectly worn mitt on one hand, and ponytail pulled through her favorite baseball cap on her head. She looked around to see her powerhouse friends next to her, and she knew this would be a season to remember.

CHAPTER 11

Jalyn

As Jalyn sat on the plane back from California, she replayed everything from the past few days back in her mind.

The event was more than Jalyn could have ever imagined. Not only was there a fancy awards ceremony, where each award winner was called up to the stage and presented a fancy trophy consisting of a gold-looking paper and pen, but they read off a summary of each story and presented them with a professional printed copy of our story. It was a dream come true to see her story wrapped around the pages of a professional-printed paperback. They found out later that book publishers might be contacting them to publish their stories for real.

The expo beforehand offered writing seminars, speakers, book signings, and a college career expo. Jalyn's mind was swimming in ideas and information. She sent about 100 pictures to Ethan and some to her parents too. They all seemed impressed with everything, and even Grandpa found some new books to read at the expo. There were so many impressive college degree programs out there focused on writing. Jalyn could not decide which one she liked the best.

One of the most impressive things Jalyn saw was a writing camp that was held at a college in Michigan over the summer. Students had to submit writing samples, and they would select camp participants to spend the week in creative writing activities, instructional sessions, and they would even have professionals at the camp to help provide insight and guidance on their writing samples. The experience sounded amazing, and Jalyn set her sights on getting accepted for that program this next summer.

Things felt right. She could only imagine how this trip might have changed her life. She leaned over the arm of her plane seat and thanked her grandfather for taking her on the trip. She knew it could not have been easy convincing her parents to let her go.

Her grandfather settled into his seat and smiled. "Did I ever tell you the story of a son who went outside the family's business to start his own grocery store?"

"Yes, grandpa...you did. That's what started this all. Remember?"

Grandpa smiled, "But this part is worth repeating...That boy's parents did not support his decision because they thought it was too risky - and it was - nothing about the future is ever guaranteed, but he knew it was what he was meant to do. So he did it. And do you know how he knew it was meant to be, Jalyn."

"How, grandpa?" Jalyn knew the answer, but she wanted to hear him say again.

"Because he was a Chibuzo, and he knew that if he gave his life and dreams and wishes to God, then God would give him the directions. Never forget that, Granddaughter. This is not the last challenge you will face in your life."

Jalyn leaned her head against his shoulder and listened as he went into all the details of his story. How he took a risk and worked incredibly hard to make it pay off. He was inspiring and passionate. He had such a glow to him as he told his story to Jalyn. While she knew this story well, she never tired of hearing all the details of her grandparents' start in the business. She was always blown away by their courage and perseverance.

"Grandpa, that's my favorite story."

"Jalyn, you have a strong fight in you. I was the same way back in the day. Your parents will come around to accept who you want to be. They just want what is best for you, but I don't doubt that you will be successful no matter what you do. Just promise me - wherever your future takes you, whatever job you choose, just be the best you can be. Everything else will fall into place." At that, her grandfather closed his eyes and fell asleep.

Jalyn took a deep breath and relaxed. She knew the future was uncertain with no exact answers, and that thought excited her. No matter what, she would be ready.

When she arrived home, the memory of her parent's concern and her nervousness was long gone. All that remained was a bright glow of possibilities and potential. Even her parents seemed more onboard and interested in all Jalyn had learned about the field of writing.

Jalyn could not wait to tell Ethan all about it. Before she could even head up the stairs, Jalyn's mom stopped her because she had noticed the difference in her. "You are positively glowing!"

Jalyn, your dad and I were talking, why don't you invite Ethan over for dinner tonight. We would like to get to know him better. She could not believe her ears. She ran upstairs to call Ethan right away.

Ethan sat and listened to Jalyn as she went through all the details of her exciting trip. She was out of breath by the end and just grabbed her pillow and screamed with excitement.

"Ethan this is the most amazing feeling. I feel so good. I feel so me. Oh, by the way, my parents wanted to know if you could come over for dinner tonight. They would like to get to know you better. I figured it might be a welcome distraction while you want to get the results of the election tomorrow," she paused, "Great! See you at 6 p.m. sharp. Please don't be late. My parents are very...punctual people."

With that Jalyn leaned back and closed her eyes. "Thank you for everything, God. I know this has everything to do with you." She leaned into the calm silence and heard a voice from within herself.

"All of this was inside of me all along. I guess I am alright."

Jalyn knew she wasn't alone. She had her God, her family, her friends, and she had Ethan. After all, he was the one who taught her that life wasn't about being perfect. It was about being real.

Ethan

Ethan took a deep breath and knocked on the door. The silence was broken by the sound of footsteps heading his way. Ethan's heart reached out when he saw Jalyn coming toward him. Ethan knew Jalyn's parents were not exactly thrilled about their friendship, but tonight was a big step. Ethan wasn't sure he could handle too many more "big steps" this week.

"Ethan, don't be nervous. Just be yourself." She snuck in a quick kiss before leading him into the kitchen where her parents sat organizing dinner.

"Dr. and Mrs. Chibuzo, thank you so much for having me over to dinner." He gave them the bouquet he bought for Jalyn's parents. "And, Jalyn, this is for you." Ethan handed her a smaller bouquet that she knew came from their field by their pond.

"They are perfect. Thank you so much, Ethan! Here, Mom, I'll add the flowers to a vase of water."

Dr. Chibuzo asked Ethan to go help him get the food off the grill, while Jalyn stayed inside and helped her mom finish the rest of dinner. Once everything was set, they sat down together.

Dinner felt like the debates all over again. He put himself out there and hoped for the best. Luckily, there was so much for them to talk about since Jalyn had just returned from her trip, and Ethan had the election results coming out tomorrow.

After dinner, Jalyn asked her parents if she and Ethan could walk to go get some ice cream. They agreed and the two headed out.

They both had so much to share, but first Ethan needed to take a deep breath. "Man, if I can survive the debates and dinner with your parents, I definitely can handle anything that comes my way." They laughed, and he held Jalyn's hand in his. "I have so much to tell you!" Jalyn went on to tell him all about her trip and her grandfather and all the exciting people she had met. "I guess we both have had some exciting days, huh?!"

The two of them sat there lost in conversation at a small booth at the local ice cream shop. Any place with Jalyn had become a special place: a place to talk, a place to sit quietly, a safe place for them to discover who they were on the inside and who they were together.

"Jalyn, there is something I have been meaning to ask you," Ethan was not quite sure how to begin; this was a topic he never really talked about out loud. "I know you talk about God and faith, and that's important to you. But I just don't understand that commitment you have...to something...to something you can't see. I have never really given God a second thought because I had, what I thought, was a shitty life. My mom doesn't talk much about religion, so I guess it was never important to me."

Jalyn smiled and squeezed Ethan's hand, "I get what you are saying 100%. My family is religious, but it has always been quite formal. I guess that is the right way to describe it in my life. Church and scripture were rules to follow. I can't say I truly understood the spiritual side of it all until recently. I prayed, just like I was supposed to. My grandpa challenged me to talk to God about my life, my struggles…like really talk to Him. It's hard to explain, but that made all the difference. God is a big part of my life and happiness." She pauses searching for the words, "Think about it this way. You love your mom, right?"

"Of course."

"Well, how do you know? You can't see 'love', no one could see you standing next to your mom and see the love between you."

"No, I guess not. But love is a feeling, not something you can see," Ethan responded.

"Exactly. I feel and know my connection with God. He has always been there for me, for all of us. But it wasn't until I started asking for him to come into my life, until I opened my heart to him, that I truly felt, and to some degree, heard him in my life. It's an amazing thing. Ethan, I can't even explain how amazing it is. But it is so hard to talk about with other people. Now I have this amazing relationship with God, and it feels nothing at all like judgment, nothing at all like grading. It is this overwhelming feeling of acceptance and love. There really aren't words to describe it. "

"Wow, that coming from someone who wants to be a writer," he teased. "I don't know if I have ever felt anything that strong in my life. I guess because my dad was so shitty to me, I never really thought I was worth God's time."

"God is our Father - each of us. He loves us beyond measure. You have always had an amazing Father in your life. Maybe you can try... what I did? Just start talking to Him."

Ethan was a little uncertain at this proposal, but he appreciated Jalyn opening up to him. He wasn't quite sure what to say next. Luckily he didn't have to say anything.

Jalyn pulled Ethan close. "Listen, mister, no matter what happens with the election, I am so proud of you. You did it. You did everything you wanted to do. You're going places, Mr. Waltz," she smiled and winked at him. "Have you ever thought about going into politics? You definitely have the guts to do it. That's for sure!"

"One office at a time, Jalyn. One office at a time."

At that moment Ethan leaned in and kissed Jalyn. He couldn't help it. She had been so close to him, close to his body, and close to his heart.

Jalyn kissed him back and they were lost in their moment together. When Jalyn leaned back she smiled.

The next morning Ethan woke up brewing with excitement, nervousness, and whatever else was in that cocktail of emotions in his stomach. Today the results of the election would be announced. Today he would find out what happened. He opened the door and walked out into the day....ready for whatever would come.

Eight hours later, as Ethan returned home from school that day, he knew full well his mom would be sitting at the kitchen table, pissed that he had ignored her texts all day long. He couldn't help it. Some news had to be delivered in person.

As he opened that same door that he left just 8 hours earlier, there she was, sitting at the table biting her nails and waiting for Ethan.

"Ethan, is your phone working? Do you know how stressful today was? Never mind. Tell me! Tell me! What happened? I am dying here!" Her eyes begged for some sort of reaction from her son.

Ethan looked up and smiled, "We did it. I got it. I am going to be class president!" She screamed and grabbed him in a monster hug.

As they hugged tears rolled down their cheeks. Somehow this victory was not just Ethan's win, but a victory for his mom as well. She had won her son back, and he was as amazing as she always knew he could be.

"Mom, I got you something. He fumbled through his bag and pulled out a small box. "This is for you."

Ethan's mom couldn't believe her eyes. "What is this?"

"Just open it!" Ethan pushed it closer to her. As she opened the box, she saw it contained a delicate ring that looked like it had the letter T on it. "What is this, Ethan? It's beautiful. Is it a cross? What does it stand for?"

Ethan paused, and his heart warmed. "I guess it is a cross." He said, confused. When he bought the ring all he could see was the sideways letter 'T', but now he could clearly see that it is a sideways cross. "It represents you," he broke off. "You see, Jalyn made up this word, ticity. It means happiness, but happiness that comes from being real and living the life you were meant to live. You have sacrificed so much for me, Mom. You helped me find ticity, and I wanted you to have it on your finger so you never forget. Thank you for standing by me through - well - everything.

His mom was speechless. She just gave him another hug, and he could feel the tears flowing again onto his shoulder.

This day was more than Ethan could have imagined. As he sat at the kitchen table, he told his mom everything about today. She listened as he told her about waiting to hear the announcements, sweating as they read through all the underclassmen winners first, hearing his name, and his classmates cheering for him. He told her about his congratulatory meeting with the principal, and he even told her about the kiss he gave Jalyn after school when she came running into his arms.

"I knew it!" It seemed to be a sweet, sweet victory for his mom too. She had known all along there was something special between him and Jalyn.

"Mom, I owe you everything."

"Ethan, you owe me nothing. You are living the life you were meant to have. You found a purpose in life. You found a way to understand who you are, even in the face of challenges. You are so strong. Stronger than you even know- with a wonderful future ahead of you. Everyone at your school can see it too. That's why they want you to represent them. They admire your glow. You radiate an authentic spirit, and people are drawn to that."

Ethan hugged his Mom, and headed upstairs to take in everything from today. "What a roller coaster!" He said to himself, and he let the memories of this past school year flood his mind.

Then he sat quietly and started, "Dear God…"

Maddie

"Bottom of the sixth, score is tied up: Westwood High 12, Highland High 12, and Lopez is up to pitch with the top of the order coming up." Maddie looked up at the announcers' booth and smirked. She loved nothing more than being the one in charge of a do-or-die situation in softball. These were the moments she loved.

Maddie scrapped at the mound with her spike, after a few warmup pitches, she was ready to go. The first batter walked up to the mound, looking at her coach for signs. Maddie, too, looked at her catcher. Fast ball down the middle, "Gottcha!"

Maddie leans back and pitches the only way she knew how - all in. Strike!

"Haha," Maddie loved this part. She gets ready for the next pitch and looks right in the eyes of the batter. She's nervous, Maddie can tell. She looks for the sign, changeup. Maddie almost laughs out loud.

And the changeup, "Strike two!" the umpire yells.

Maddie doesn't even need a sign for the next pitch. She's pitched against this batter many times. Low fast pitch to the inside, and, "Strike three!"

"See ya!" Maddie said to herself with a laugh.

Maddie's game of sizing up batters goes on for only two more batters, ending the inning with a tied score. This situation would make most high school players nervous, but the more on the line, the more Maddie rose to the challenge. She knew the score of the game never meant *that* much. It was just a game, after all.

As Maddie walked into the dugout still riding her high, she hears, "Lopez, you're on deck."

Her team was right by her side, "Go, Lopez, go!" and "You got this, girl!"

She was ready. She stepped up next to the batter's box, leaned back to take a sign from her coach, did a few full swings, tapped the insides of her spikes, and pointed the bat right at the pitcher. As she waited to settle into the batter's box, she was flooded with a feeling of gratitude. Everything just felt right at the moment. She was so happy. "No," she smiled to herself. She was feeling ticity at this moment. "Thank you, Jalyn!" she said to herself as she settled into the batter's box, ready for the pitch.

Her coach's rule was to always take the first pitch. "Strike one!"

She barely moved, "Game on, sucker!" She gave the pitcher her biggest smile.

The pitch was out, Maddie looked, and SMACK! The ball flew out to center field. Flying, flying, flying...it's over the fence! Maddie's first homerun of the season.

She ran around the bases, touched home, and hugged her teammates. She couldn't help but let one tear escape her eye. Her team and the fans were all cheering. There was nothing better than entering the dugout after a home run, out of breath, and covered in dust. She high-fived everyone there and walked out to high-five her parents.

As she walked to the stands, a man stopped her. "Maddie, it's a pleasure to meet you. I am Coach Balister, and I coach the Lady Rockets at WAJC. You are playing one heck of a game. I will certainly be keeping an eye on your next two seasons here at Westwood High."

"Thank you, coach," Maddie responded without a thought.

"I'll see you around, Miss Lopez."

Maddie's parents were the next two people she saw. She hugged them without words because they knew…they knew.

After winning the game, Maddie went for a victory dinner with the team at The Diner. That's what it was called, simply The Diner. It was Westwood's best family restaurant in town. They served the biggest mound of the most crispy fries in town. There was nothing better than downing a plateful of The Diner fries covered in cheese and ketchup after a sweet win over Highland.

On her way home from dinner, Maddie saw a text from Jalyn. "Bonfire at Ethan's. Be there!"

There was no better end to the day Maddie just had than a sweet, sweet s'mores at Ethan's. Maddie knew that Ms. Waltz would have every ingredient needed to make the best s'mores ever!

"Hey, ya'll!" Maddie joked as she entered the party. Jalyn came running up to her. "Holy crap, girl. That game was seriously stressful! I think I aged 10 years just watching it!"

"Nah, I knew our girl Maddie had it taken care of," Ethan added smoothly.

"I am glad you did!" Maddie added with a slug to Ethan's shoulder.

"So, what are we serving tonight?" Maddie asked, fully ready to judge.

"Oh, Ms. Waltz??" Maddie disappeared into the house as Ethan leaned over and kissed Jalyn.

"Would you be okay with me telling you I love you?" Ethan whispered to Jalyn.

She tilted her head back and looked deep into his eyes. "If you say it, Mr. Waltz, you better mean it." She leaned in and kissed Ethan with every inch of her.

After they were done kissing, Jalyn put her forehead to Ethan's and whispered, "I love you too." Time stood still as Ethan and Jalyn stood, foreheads together, eyes closed, and arms entangled behind Jalyn's back. They wished time could stand still.

But unfortunately, there were other people there who started chanting, "S'mores queen, s'mores queen, s'mores queen!" Jalyn looked up to see Maddie dancing down to the bonfire with Ms. Waltz, plates full of s'mores ingredients.

Ethan and Jalyn just laughed.

"Okay, who's ready for some creative s'mores," Ms. Waltz asked. Maddie posted a huge blackboard with at least 10 different s'mores combinations.

Everyone twisted and turned, grabbed and poked to get the ingredients they wanted. After everyone got a turn to make their s'mores, Ethan, Maddie and Jalyn met at the fire.

"Okay, so what is everyone eating?" Ethan asked. "I am cooking the *choco-banana marsh*: chocolate bar, banana slices, graham cracker, and marshmallow."

Jalyn chimed in, "I, sir, prefer the minty meltaway: mint chocolate bar with marshmallows and graham crackers. How about you, Maddie?"

Everyone waited for Chef Maddie's recommendation. "So mine is a little different. I have a graham cracker and marshmallow combined with a chocolate peanut butter bar and just a touch of strawberry jelly."

They laughed as the jelly dripped down Maddie's chin and she licked it up.

"Can you believe we are going to be seniors next year?" Jalyn asked.

"Are we even mature enough to be seniors?" Maddie laughed and tossed her head back.

"I don't know about you, but I am so ready for senior year," Ethan boasted as he pretended to act like he was the king of the fire.

Everyone around him threw marshmallows at him, and laughed, and laughed.

Finally, Ethan rose from the assault of marshmallows and raised his skewer…

"To ticity…" Maddie and Jalyn smiled at each other with an all-knowing smile, "To ticity!"

ABOUT THE AUTHOR

Jennie Stiglic has always known her superpower was writing and communications. After working in public relations and as a business writer, Stiglic turned her attention to teaching. Since then, she has worked as an English teacher for more than a decade.

Her students have inspired her to look for ways to empower and guide the next generation. In an airbrushed and electronic world, kids need a voice of strength and trust in their lives. They need to know that their only expectations for life should be their own.

Made in the USA
Monee, IL
02 December 2024

72022364R00125